"You

Katie turned and gasped in alarm when she suddenly found herself staring at a man standing at the end of the bar. "I didn't know anyone was here."

The man blinked at her in surprise. "You can see me?"

Katie laughed. "I know it's dark in here, but you're too big to miss. Are you a tourist? I didn't see any cars outside."

"No," he said with a shake of his head.

"You can't possibly live here."

"But I do."

"How odd," she said. "I've come to this ghost town before but I've never seen you."

A strange smile twisted his lips. "I try to stay out of people's way." As if he'd had a choice. For the past hundred years he hadn't been seen or spoken to by anybody. Who was this beautiful woman, and why was she able to break one hundred years of silence?

Dear Reader,

This month, a new "Rising Star" comes out to shine as American Romance continues to search the heavens for the best new talent...the best new stories.

Let me introduce you to Kim Hansen.

A lover of the West and its wild and wonderful history, Kim found bringing a sheriff from the past forward in time the perfect way to bring a bit of history into the present, where riding off into the sunset is only a remembered phrase instead of a literal event.

Turn the page...and Catch a "Rising Star"!

Sincerely,

Debra Matteucci
Senior Editor & Editorial Coordinator
Harlequin Books
300 East 42nd St.
New York, NY 10017

Kim Hansen

TIME RAMBLER

Harlequin Books

TORONTO • NEW YORK • LONDON
AMSTERDAM • PARIS • SYDNEY • HAMBURG
STOCKHOLM • ATHENS • TOKYO • MILAN
MADRID • WARSAW • BUDAPEST • AUCKLAND

To Mom and Dad
for always being there,
and to Kathy and Jodi
for always believing

ISBN 0-373-16548-X

TIME RAMBLER

Copyright © 1994 by Kim Hansen.

This edition published by arrangement with Harlequin Enterprises B. V.

® and TM are trademarks of the publisher. Trademarks indicated with
® are registered in the United States Patent and Trademark Office, the
Canadian Trade Marks Office and in other countries.

Printed in U.S.A.

Prologue

Montana, Spring—1883

"How much farther, Mama?"

Molly Hunnicutt smiled down at her five-year-old son. Already he was the mirror image of his father. Blond hair, brown eyes and a stubborn streak as wide as it was long. But he also had a smile that could melt her heart. "Not very, Billy." She immediately looked to the man sitting on the buckboard seat on the other side of Billy for confirmation.

Tall and long of limb, Travis McCord was her husband's best friend—as well as the man *her* best friend was sure she was in love with. Annie Bernhardt was mad for Eagle River's sheriff, and as Travis sent Molly one of his easy smiles, she could well understand why. Even in the shade of the broad-brimmed Stetson he wore, Travis McCord had the bluest eyes she'd ever seen. He also had a set of broad shoulders, a deep voice and a warm and friendly manner that could charm even the most violent-tempered men in the district into dropping their fists—or their guns—when he asked. A rueful smile twisted Molly's lips. If she hadn't been married already, Travis McCord would have been a man she, too, would have sought after.

"Just a few more minutes," Travis told her and looked down to Billy. "You want to take the team the rest of the way to Tyler's?"

"Yeah!" Billy exclaimed and eagerly sat forward as Travis expertly transferred the reins of the two-horse team into his smaller hands.

Molly shook her head. Travis was good with children. He was good with everybody. But while he was always polite and courteous to the women of Eagle River, he wasn't ready to marry any of them. Still, he was young yet. When he'd arrived in Eagle River two years earlier to take control of the booming mining and cattle town, he'd just crossed into his mid-twenties.

Travis looked up to find Molly watching him. A small woman with auburn hair and hazel eyes, she wore a blue gingham dress, and an expression of worry. "He'll be all right," he quickly assured her, glancing down at Billy as the boy gleefully "guided" the horses down the straight if bumpy road to their destination.

"I wasn't thinking about him. I was thinking about you."

Travis felt uncomfortable heat burn its way up his neck under her observant stare. Molly was the one person in Eagle River who could make him feel like a schoolboy instead of a man, but she was also someone he admired.

Leaving a comfortable home and her family behind, she'd gone with her husband and infant son into the wilds of Montana to build a home. Life hadn't been and often still wasn't easy, but Molly never complained. Her love for and trust in her husband was absolute, and her loyalty was something Travis both respected and envied. Molly was the type of woman he wished for, but she already belonged to his best friend. Travis accepted that and had no desire to change it. Some day he would find someone to call his own.

"Steve would have come—"

"If he could," she interrupted. "I know. But today the cows took precedence."

Travis grinned. "They may not be as pretty as you—"

"But they bring a better price at market. I know." Abruptly they both began to laugh. "You two sound more and more alike each day."

"Sound is all."

Molly turned surprised eyes on him, but Travis wasn't looking at her. He was looking away from the buckboard to the rolling land beyond. "Is that envy I hear?" she prodded gently.

His smile was sheepish. "He's doing what I'd like to."

"Ranch?" And, at his nod, "Then why don't you?"

Travis shrugged. "You don't ranch for yourself. You do it for a family—build it for a family. A ranch is no place to live alone."

"There are plenty of women in town who'd be happy to help you make a home if that's what you're looking for."

He grinned at the look in her dancing hazel eyes. "Like Annie?"

Molly grimaced. "Is she that obvious?"

Travis shrugged in good-natured acceptance. "Women tend to like a man they see as a hero, and too many folks hereabout are still thanking me for 'saving their town.'"

"Maybe it's the man they like and not the badge."

"Maybe, but I'm not sure I'm ready to give it up yet. I need to get myself a little money before trying to settle down." His smile flashed again. "I could try to find myself a pot of gold."

Molly snorted in unladylike distaste. "Become a miner?"

"Who knows? With a little luck, I could end up like Tyler."

"Tyler's rich!" Billy put in, not looking away from the horses and proving, as always, that he was listening to every word being said around him.

"Rich in the head," Molly objected. "If Tyler Fenton had all the gold he's always bragging about, he wouldn't be living in a run-down shack, and we wouldn't be going out with some food to make sure he doesn't starve to death."

Travis sat back in the seat and put one long leg up on the wagon box in front of him. "He is a mystery. Swears he's just waiting for the right day and the right cause to put his gold on."

"Do you think there's any truth to any of his stories?"

"Tyler's lived here an awful long time. He was here before the town was." Travis met her eyes over Billy's head. "I suppose he could have found and stashed some away, but with all the time I've spent talking and visiting with him, I've never seen anything to make me believe he really struck it rich."

"Mrs. Parker says Tyler's an old fool who's lived alone too long," Billy piped up.

Molly rolled her eyes at Travis. Mrs. Parker was a busybody who spent more time gossiping than she did anything else.

"She says she can't understand why I don't have a baby brother or sister yet either," Billy added.

Molly gasped, and Travis choked as he tried to smother a bark of laughter.

"Mrs. Parker should mind her own business!" Molly snapped as her cheeks burned, all too aware that Travis was pointedly looking anywhere but at her.

"There's Tyler's place up ahead," Travis announced a bit too loudly. "I hope he's home."

"Where else would he be?" Molly grumbled.

Travis grinned at her but quickly turned his attention to helping Billy guide the horses to a stop just off the road. When the buckboard came to a halt, Travis jumped down to tie the horses to a broken fence post and turned to survey the yard beyond.

The house, or more accurately shack, Tyler lived in was small and ramshackle. Its roof was bowed, but the walls were sound. The so-called barn behind it wasn't much better, but the one corral housing two long-eared mules was in good repair.

Travis noted the open door to the shack and let out a yell. "Yo, Tyler! You have visitors!"

Nobody answered.

"Tyler!"

"You think he might not be here?" Molly asked from the seat of the buckboard.

"Not likely," Travis assured her. "Both mules are in the corral. Maybe he's in the barn. He doesn't hear too well anymore." Turning back to the wagon seat, Travis reached up to help first Billy, then Molly to the ground. "I'll go out back and look."

"Maybe he's checking on his gold!" Billy told Travis, eyes wide.

Travis smiled and reached down to ruffle the blond hair on Billy's head. "Maybe." He looked at Molly, whose head barely reached his shoulder. "I'll be right back."

Molly nodded and, as he walked away, got her son's attention before he could race off. "Billy, why don't you climb up in back and hand me down the basket?"

Travis crossed the yard with long-legged strides that ate up the distance to the barn. It was a quiet spring day. The sky was blue, the sun bright, and the buds of the season had burst into bloom. Leaves whispered on the trees, and wildflowers raced across the countryside and over the hill behind the cabin in wild abandon. The natural beauty surrounding the battered buildings Tyler Fenton owned made Travis wonder again about the old man's claims of wealth.

If Tyler did have the gold he always boasted of, it would have been an easy thing to turn his ramshackle abode into a ranch most men could only dream of. The grass grew rich and thick in the meadows nearby, and a stream that ran full and fresh all year cut through the property. Travis just couldn't believe that if Tyler had the money to spend, he wouldn't use it to make the place into all it could be.

"Tyler?" Travis called as he approached the open door of the barn. He paused and stepped inside with the caution born of years of carrying a gun and wearing a badge, but no sound greeted him as he moved out of the light to stand next to the door. "Tyler?"

Again no one answered, and Travis frowned. Where could the old prospector be? It was dark in the barn, and Travis had to let his eyes adjust before moving down the aisle. His hand lingered close to the butt of the Colt in the holster strapped around his hips, but thoughts of the weapon and danger abruptly vanished when he saw a man lying in a heap on the floor.

With an oath, Travis fell to his knees beside Tyler. The old man was lying in a puddle of his own blood. Travis searched for a pulse but found none. Tyler Fenton was dead, but not by accident. Somebody had hit him over the head. And recently. His body was still warm.

Suddenly a shot exploded outside. "Molly!" The echo of his cry followed Travis out of the barn as he leapt to his feet and into a run. Without conscious thought he grabbed the Colt, and his finger automatically tightened on the trigger as a man appeared around the side of the shack.

Travis and the stranger saw each other at the same time. They both raised their guns. Both fired. Travis ducked and felt a bullet whistle past him, but the stranger staggered as he was hit. Gamely the man tried to raise his weapon for a second shot, but his knees gave out and he collapsed into the dirt.

Travis didn't stop moving. Having slowed to shoot, he started running again, and his insides twisted when he heard Billy wail. Travis skidded around the corner of the shack, his gun still ready, but the breath left him when he saw Molly sprawled on the ground.

Blood was spreading across her pretty gingham dress. Billy was on his knees beside her, tears streaking his face, and the picnic basket filled with food was dumped upside down nearby. Travis's heart leapt into his throat as time seemed to stand still, and he caught a motion out of the corner of his eye. A man stood in the doorway. He had a gun raised and aimed. As Travis watched, the six-gun the outlaw was holding

spit lead. Travis tried to dodge as he returned the
gunfire, but he wasn't quick enough. The bullet caught
and knocked him backward, spinning him around.

He crashed to the dirt as the world heaved around
him, and pain exploded inside his head. Blood mush-
roomed across his shirt and his gun dropped from
suddenly nerveless fingers as a black wave threatened
to wash over him. But his thoughts weren't for himself. They were for Molly. How was he going to tell
Steve about Molly?

Chapter One

Montana, Spring—1994

The Jeep stopped at the old hitching post, looking sadly out of place in the middle of the dead Western town. Tumbleweeds were the only other "vehicles" parked on the street, and no one else was in sight as Katie Shannon stepped from behind the wheel and onto the dusty road that wagon wheels had once marked.

Removing her sunglasses and tossing them on the dashboard, she squinted against the sun's glare and took a deep breath. The smell of rotting wood combined with dirt and dust rushed to assault her senses, but it was a welcome invasion. She enjoyed the flavor of the scents. She was used to them, and a smile curved her lips as her eyes caressed the row of broken-down buildings that reflected a time and age long gone by.

The general store, the cobbler shop, the telegraph office, the jail. She'd been in each one countless times. Her first visit had been as a little girl when her father had brought her, but one look was all it had taken to fascinate and captivate her for the rest of her life.

Walking around the Jeep to the boardwalk, her shadow stretched out before her as she climbed the creaking steps to the hardware store. Living on a ranch nearby, she could stop by the old town whenever she wanted, but it was rare that she ever saw anyone else when she did. An occasional tourist, maybe, but they always saw the town as dead. To her, it was still alive—with the memories and the dreams of those who had once walked its streets.

Slowly she moved down the boardwalk, looking through broken and dirty windows to the empty interiors of stores and shops. The barber and blacksmith, the seamstress and schoolteacher. They had all made their homes in Eagle River—until the gold had run out and the railroad had gone north instead of south.

Katie stopped to look in the barbershop. The loss of the miners hadn't hurt much. The ranchers and their families could have kept Eagle River alive, but when the railroad had turned away from the town and taken the goods everyone needed and wanted with it, shops had begun to close and homes had been deserted until only ghosts had remained to keep the town alive.

With a sigh Katie moved on, stuffing her hands into the pockets of her worn blue jeans as she walked and looked at the remnants of a town left to die.

Beyond the city limits the ranchers had stayed on, buying up any extra land to increase their herds and betting that civilization wouldn't always be so far away. And, they'd been right. Slowly, roads had been built, cars had replaced wagons and the town had come back into reach. But, too late. Eagle River had already died. Everyone had gone.

Katie followed the boardwalk to another building where colored glass lined the windows and swinging doors hung drunkenly on rusted hinges. The town saloon. She smiled and stepped inside. This was where

people had come to have fun and where the warm
sensation of happy times still lingered in the air. She
walked forward to the bar with its tarnished rails and
battered countertop, totally oblivious to the dust and
cobwebs and the dust particles dancing happily in the
sunlight trailing across the floor.

She stopped to stare at the broken piano in the corner. While its music had played, rowdy cowboys and
miners had whirled dance-hall girls across the floor,
and men had placed bets on a turn of a card, a toss of
the dice or the spin of a wheel. Her eyes skipped from
the ceiling and its dusty chandeliers to the broken ta-
bles and the lopsided chairs scattered across the floor.
How much simpler life had been then. How much less
complicated. Unlike today. Unlike now. For her.

She turned and gasped in alarm when she suddenly
found herself staring at a man. Standing at the end of
the bar, he was tall and dark and completely silent.

"You startled me!" she told him, her heart lurch-
ing back into place beneath her rib cage. "I didn't
know anyone else was here."

The man blinked at her in surprise. "You can see
me?"

Katie laughed. "I know it's dark in here, but you're
too big to miss and too solid to be a ghost." And, he
was big, though just about everyone was to her. At
five foot two, she had to look up to almost all she met
except children. But her stature had nothing to do with
the startling strength of his appearance.

Just about six foot, his shoulders filled out his
rough cotton shirt with determined strength, and his
legs were long and steady over scuffed boots. But, it
was the blue of his eyes that attracted her. His gaze
seemed to reach out and surround her with an intense

longing, as if he was a thirsty man and she a glass of water. He needed her, and Katie didn't stop to think why. She just reacted.

"Are you visiting? A tourist? I didn't see any other cars outside."

"No," he finally managed with a shake of his head.

Katie smiled, attracted by his self-conscious manner that made him seem baffled, happy and wary all at once. "You can't possibly live here."

"But I do."

She stopped to stare at him and suddenly became more aware of the details of his attire. He wore a leather vest over his cotton shirt with what looked remarkably like a tin badge, and a gun belt was strapped around his hips. The Colt sitting in the holster looked incredibly real. Her eyes went back to his face, lean and dark under the wide-brimmed Stetson he wore. "For how long?"

His gaze left her to sweep the room, and she was touched by an aura of sadness. "Too long."

"You're the caretaker?"

He looked back at her, startled by the question. Caretaker. That's what a sheriff was. It was what he had been. But why was she asking him that? How could she ask him anything? Was he dreaming? "I guess you could say that."

"How odd," she said, and stuffed her hands into the front pockets of her jeans. "I come here quite a bit, and I've never seen you before."

A strange smile twisted his lips. "I try to stay out of people's way." As if he'd had a choice until this woman had come and suddenly started talking to him! Travis stared at her. For the past hundred years he hadn't been seen or spoken to by anybody. Not since the day Molly had died, and he'd shot to kill and been shot himself.

Travis frowned as he went over, again, the last few minutes of his life. The bullet had caught him as he'd tried to dive out of the way, after he'd seen Molly lying lifeless on the ground with little Billy wailing beside her. But instead of following her to a grave, he'd ended up in some type of purgatory.

Waking from a blackness that had been like none other he'd ever experienced, he'd suddenly found himself standing in the cemetery watching Steve Hunnicutt bury Molly. Billy had been clinging tightly to Steve's hand and most of the town had been present, but when he'd tried to talk to Steve, to tell him how sorry he was, Steve had walked right past him—as had everyone else.

Sick at heart, Travis had thought they'd all been angry because he'd let Steve down. Steve had trusted him to take care of Molly, and he hadn't. Because of him, Molly had died. But then he'd seen the second grave and the marker with his name on it. He'd kind of passed out then, and he'd been waking up and nodding out again ever since.

"It must be lonely."

Travis's attention came back to her. To the first person to speak directly to him, to actually see him, in . . . how long? "It has been." He watched a bright smile curve her lips and light hazel eyes.

"Past tense," she said. "I'll take that as a compliment." Katie turned to walk to one of the saloon windows overlooking the street. Most of the panes had somehow remained unbroken. "You must like the old West, too. It's always fascinated me. When I was a little girl I used to come here and dream about what it must have been like when people lived here. It must have been exciting.''

Travis watched her walk away, his eyes following her slim form. She was short and petite with blond hair that swept her shoulders, and she was dressed for the times. Like the other women he'd seen come and go, she wore blue jeans and a light cotton shirt instead of a gingham dress or blouse and skirt. Women still wore dresses. Not the kind he recognized, but they wore dresses—although sometimes they wore a lot less. Bare legs, bare arms, bare midriffs. He'd been shocked by the lack of attire at first, but he'd gotten used to it. He'd had to. Travis followed the young woman to the window, afraid to let her get too far away from him. He didn't want to be alone anymore. ''It had its moments.''

She threw a smile over her shoulder. ''You sound as if you were there.''

Travis looked away from her and out the window to the deserted street. ''I was.'' From beginning to end he'd been there, flashing in and out of the town for a day here, an hour there, as time had seen Eagle River go from a thriving city to a ghost town.

She watched him stare out the grimy glass panes, again overwhelmed by a sense of his aloneness.

''Place has seen a lot of changes. Lots of people have come and gone.''

''I wish I'd known them.''

Travis turned at the strength of her declaration and found her frowning at the bar.

She turned to him again and smiled at his puzzled stare. ''It's just that so much of them has been left behind.''

He shook his head. ''I don't understand.''

"You must!" Katie insisted. "Otherwise you wouldn't be working here." He looked uncertain, and she hurried to explain. "Don't you feel it sometimes? The town may look dead on the outside, but inside it's still alive. The memories, the hopes. The people may have moved away, but their dreams didn't go with them. They built something here, and when they moved on, they left part of themselves behind." She stared into the room almost as if she was watching for something. "Sometimes it's as if you can hear them talking, see them walking. You just have to stand real still."

A slow smile spread across his mouth. "Some people'd say you were seeing ghosts."

A soft flush filled her cheeks and, embarrassed by his steady gaze, she shrugged. "No, they just tell me I have an overactive imagination." Suddenly she pulled a hand from her pocket to hold it out to him. "My name's Katie Shannon. I live not too far from here."

For a moment Travis only stared at her hand. He was afraid to take it. He'd tried to touch people before, to get their attention, but it had never worked. It wasn't like a ghost tale where he could move through objects or objects could move through him. It was just a lack of substance. When he tried to touch people, they just didn't feel it. And worse, he couldn't feel them. Yet when his fingers closed over hers, the warmth of her palm met his, and the tide of relief that hit him almost buckled his knees. He could feel! "Travis McCord."

"McCord..." Her fingers tightened on his. "Why, there was a sheriff by that name who used to live here! His grave is up on the hill just outside of town!" She pulled her hand from his with an embarrassed shrug. "But you probably already know that."

Travis clenched his hands into fists to resist the urge to reach out and touch her again. Not only could she see and talk to him, she could touch him, too!

"You probably know all the names up there," Katie went on.

"I know that and a lot more."

"Like who they were and what they did?"

"And where they lived."

Katie didn't understand the sadness in his tone, but she was too excited at the prospect of finding the answers to the questions she'd had for years to really notice. "Can you show me? Give me a tour? I mean, that's what a caretaker does, isn't it?" Before he could say no, she grabbed his hand and was leading him out the door.

Travis abruptly found himself out on the street fielding dozens of questions. He had no more time to wonder who she was or why she, of all those he had seen over the years, was the one to finally see him again. Instead he tried to answer all she asked as he described people and events of a time gone by. If he found it strange that someone from the present was as interested in the past as he, Travis didn't give it much thought. Katie kept him too busy and, in truth, he was too glad to be able to share the memories he'd clung to for so long to question her motives.

Joyfully neighbors and friends came to life again as he spoke about them, and Travis found himself laughing along with Katie as he recalled strange habits or odd remarks. It was good to visit with those he'd known once, nice to know he wasn't lost to the realm of reality any longer, and a relief to realize he hadn't gone insane during the passage of time. He could still relate to people, tell a joke, share a tear.

Thankfully, he hadn't spent every day since his "death" waiting for someone to come to break the spell. It hadn't been his fate to spend three hundred and sixty-five days a year watching the hours pass. It had just seemed that way. In reality he didn't know how much time he'd really spent "awake" watching the years go by, but it had been enough to let him somehow keep pace with the town—and what happened miles away from it.

Through listening to people, reading magazines and newspapers left behind by those who visited Eagle River, he'd watched and learned history. Never could he pick up things in anyone's presence, but when they were gone, things of the future had become his, a man of the past. In an effort to understand the changes constantly in progress, he'd devoured guidebooks that had been dropped, watched wagons be replaced by motorized vehicles called cars, vans and trucks and learned that the once-whispered-about conveniences of electricity, plumbing and telephones had become widespread reality.

Yet seeing and reading about it had never been enough. He'd wanted to ask questions, understand more, but that hadn't been possible. The only thing that he completely knew for truth was why he had been condemned. Molly had died because he hadn't done his job. Instead of paying attention to all the signs that had to have been in the yard, he'd left her alone to be murdered. Molly had trusted him. So had Steve. He'd let them both down. That was why he'd been sentenced to a living death instead of finding the peace prayed for beyond the grave.

Yet as he watched Katie walk beside him, Travis realized his exile had apparently ended. He was no longer alone, no longer condemned to silence and bitter reflection. Katie Shannon had come to change all that. He was free. He didn't know why he had suddenly been pardoned, but he'd never been one to question good fortune.

Katie led the way from the boardwalks to the hill beyond the town and the cemetery. "I can't believe all you know is in some history book. I mean, people kept diaries and everything, but," she said, turning to look up at him, "are you sure you're not making any of this up?"

Travis made a motion across his chest. "Cross my heart and hope to die." Katie laughed, a light sound that seemed to warm him all the way to his toes. He liked this woman, this Katie. She was full of life and love for a world she had never been a part of. He followed her through the sagging gate to a headstone that read Ernest Marshall, RIP.

"Isn't this the one who fell in the water trough?" she asked.

"The very same."

"And she's the one who threw the pie at the town dance?" Katie asked, pointing to another grave marker, but after circling the small cemetery, she stopped abruptly at another grave. "This is your namesake."

Travis stared at the worn stone that sat in crooked defiance on the ground. He still didn't know what to feel when he saw his own grave, except bewilderment. He wasn't dead. Never had been. He was still breathing, walking, talking. That wasn't death. Your eyes didn't open when you were dead, your body didn't move. You didn't feel pain, and your skin wasn't warm to the touch. Steve had to have buried someone else. Not him.

"You haven't said much about Travis McCord, and he was the town sheriff."

"Not a very good one."

Katie was surprised by the anger in Travis's tone. "Why do you say that?"

"He let his best friend's wife be killed."

Katie frowned and moved to the next grave site. "Molly Hunnicutt."

Travis looked at her sharply.

"He took Molly and her son, Billy, out to see an old man who lived just outside of town," Katie said slowly. "Tyler Fenton. Molly was taking him some food. She was always worried old Tyler would starve, even though he claimed to have plenty of gold hidden somewhere." Katie stuffed her hands into her pockets. "When they got to Tyler's place he didn't answer their call, so Travis left Molly to go look for Tyler. He didn't know there were men inside the cabin. Thieves who'd killed Tyler for the gold he always talked about. Molly walked in and surprised the men. She was shot. Travis came running but too late."

"Not entirely too late. He killed one of them."

Katie frowned. "Both. He got them both." She looked up at Travis. "I would have thought you'd know that. Your namesake died a hero."

"Not a hero. If he'd been doing his job, Molly wouldn't have been killed. He would have gone in the cabin first. He would have taken the bullet." Travis fought back the anger and frustration and frowned at Katie. "How do you know so much about what happened?"

Katie smiled. "Family history. Molly's my great-great-grandmother."

Travis stared at her in disbelief, but even as he wanted to deny the truth of her statement, he saw what had been there all along. Katie looked like Molly. The hazel eyes, the small but womanly body. The hair was different, blond instead of rich auburn, and the face wasn't quite the same, but Katie Shannon had the same glow about her, the same love of life that had always filled Molly. "You look like her."

Katie's nose wrinkled. "Everyone says that."

"It's true."

She cocked her head at him. "You've seen the miniature, too?"

"I've seen the real thing."

Katie laughed. "You're as bad as I am! But I think having an imagination is a wonderful thing, don't you?"

Before Travis could comment, she turned away, but her reaction to his declaration left him baffled. Katie Shannon didn't believe he'd known Molly Hunnicutt. She didn't believe he was from the past. She just accepted his presence as if it was natural, as if he belonged, and he had nothing but his word to prove otherwise. "Do you know what happened to Steve?" he asked, following her out of the graveyard.

"Steve Hunnicutt? Yes, he stayed on with his son, Billy, after the town kind of faded away. He bought out his neighbors and managed to get a nice spread. When he died, Billy kept up the tradition."

"Steve never married again?"

"No."

Pain cut Travis like a knife. His friend had spent the rest of his life alone, without the woman he loved, because the man he had trusted to look after his wife had let him down.

"But Billy married. That's why I'm here." She grinned up at him. "Great-Grandpa Billy had a son and a daughter, and the son got the ranch. My grandfather, but he only had two daughters. My mother and Aunt Roxanne. Roxanne was the oldest, but she hated the ranch. As soon as she was old enough, she married and moved away and left my mother to inherit the Bar H when my grandparents were killed in an accident. And, my mother married David Shannon."

"Your father. He was a rancher?"

Back on the streets of town, Katie smiled. "He loved it. My mother did, too. They taught me everything they know."

"You're an only child?"

She nodded.

"And you're still ranching with them?"

Her eyes fell. "Still ranching but not with them. They're both dead."

"I'm sorry."

Katie stopped by the Jeep to stare up at him. "My father died when I was twelve. Mom and I made it alone for a while, but then she remarried. Simon Griffith. Not a rancher, but a nice man."

"You're not running the ranch alone," Travis said with a frown. "You must be married?"

"No, not yet. It's just me."

The comment was meant to be carefree, but the underlying tone was tight. And Travis didn't like the dark lines of doubt that came to touch her face and dulled the glow in her eyes. The ranch was in trouble. She was in over her head. "What's this Simon Griffith doing now your mother's gone? Is he helping?"

"Simon doesn't know the front end of a horse from the back," Katie said with a laugh. "He's a business-man. He's good at ledgers and things." She shrugged. "When Mom died he wanted me to sell, but I couldn't. There were...problems, but I'm working them out."

"Your mother died recently?"

"Not quite a year ago."

Travis didn't like the way she suddenly wouldn't meet his eyes. She was worried, afraid.

"Simon moved out of the house afterward when I decided to stay, said he was making room for my hus-band."

"You're going to be marrying?" Travis demanded, and was surprised to find the possibility alarmed him.

Katie flushed. "Nothing's been planned. I'm see-ing someone, but..." She shrugged. "It's too soon to think about. I need some time."

Oddly relieved by her answer, Travis wanted to ask more but sensed he couldn't. Katie was already with-drawing from him. He didn't want to lose her. "Can I help?"

"You've helped already." She smiled at him and then turned to look up and down the streets. "This place has always been my getaway. When I need to think or be alone, I come here. Sounds silly, I know, but I like it here. I like the...atmosphere. It's friendly."

"I'm glad."

Embarrassed by the warm intensity of his gaze, Ka-tie glanced at the watch on her wrist. "I've got to get going. As it is, Mark's going to have a fit."

"Mark?"

"My new foreman."

"What happened to the old one?" Travis asked, wondering if he had been one of those men who didn't like working for a woman.

"There was an accident," Katie told him, suddenly sad again. "His car went off the road." She bit her lip. Bill Henry had been her friend, confidant, tutor, companion ever since she could remember. "He was helping me try to straighten things out." She shook her head. "But the problems..." She gestured futilely. The problems were still there. Without Bill, she was trying to fix them alone, but it was as if the ranch had turned against her.

Travis watched her, seeing the glint of tears and feeling a fierce urge to protect her from any more hurt. His fists clenched at his sides. He'd let Molly down. He'd seen her killed in the prime of life, but he could redeem himself. He could help Molly's great-great-granddaughter keep the ranch Steve had built. That had to be why he was alive again! He was being given a second chance.

Katie abruptly swung to climb into the Jeep, and turned the keys in the ignition.

Panic hit, and Travis stepped forward to stand beside the door as she closed it. "You're leaving."

Katie was surprised by the pain in his voice and on his face. "I've really enjoyed the day, but I have to go." Her eyes were caught by his, and for a moment she clung to the strength she saw there. He seemed so big and able. It was tempting to give in to the urge to throw herself into his arms, to cling to the shoulders that appeared broad enough to carry both her and her problems with ease. "I'll be back." She was surprised that the words came out in a breathless rush.

"Soon."

She smiled. "I promise." She started to shift gears and stopped. "Would you like to see the ranch?" She didn't know what prompted the invitation, but the light that leapt into his eyes made her glad she'd made the offer.

Travis held his breath. "Yes."

"Let's see." She bit her lip. "Today's Thursday. I've got to go to town tomorrow. How about Saturday?"

"Fine."

"Ten o'clock?"

"I'll be waiting."

Katie suddenly felt incredibly happy. "Take good care of my town until then."

Travis didn't speak but stepped back as she waved and pulled away. Yet, watching her go, he was abruptly overwhelmed with fear. What if when she returned, she couldn't see him? He took a step after her, but it was too late. Her Jeep was taking her away, and he couldn't follow—didn't know where to go if he could. Was the ranch house still where it had been? How much had time changed the homestead?

Spinning on his heel, Travis strode back to the saloon and inside to the bar. She had to be able to see him when she came back. Katie Shannon needed him. More, he needed her. He needed to make right the wrong that had been done years before.

Dirt crunched beneath tires outside, and Travis spun. Katie? He hurried to the window to look, but it wasn't her. It was a family of three. Parents and their son. Tourists. Travis watched them get out of the car. If he was going to help Katie he needed to know more—not only about her and the ranch but about the times. And he needed a stake. All he had was the shirt on his back and the coins in his pocket. Somehow he had to outfit himself.

His mind whirled. The coin money he had might be worth something. Things of the past seemed to gain in value, at least according to some of the books he'd been able to grab. He'd read about antiques. His hand touched the Colt on his hip. It would be considered an antique. His fingers closed around the butt. But he couldn't give it up. Not unless he had to. The coins would have to do. He'd make them do.

Swallowing, Travis took a step toward the door. He could play caretaker again and maybe convince the tourists to give him a lift to the closest town. He'd tried to leave once, getting into a car without anyone else knowing it, but he'd passed out and into the void again before they'd gotten a mile away and woke up later back in town. Fear knotted his stomach. What if the same thing happened? How could he help Katie if he couldn't leave Eagle River? What if the tourists outside couldn't see him? If only Katie could actually see and speak to him, what good would he be to her?

Regardless, he had to try. For Katie, for Molly and Steve, and for himself. He had to at least try to get to a city, get some money and as much knowledge as he could absorb. He had to watch everything and everybody. He had to learn. Quickly. That had been part of his job as lawman. Watch and learn. A lawman's life could depend on how quickly he picked up on things around him and on how well he read people, but this time it wouldn't be just his life on the line. It would be Katie's. Travis took a deep breath and stepped outside onto the porch.

Chapter Two

Travis cringed and clung to the armrest as Earl Carter pressed a pedal to the floor and the car roared through a left turn that plastered everyone back against their seats. After seeing so many and such a variety of cars and trucks come through Eagle River over the years, he'd often wondered what riding in one of the motorized vehicles would be like, but the experience was proving to be more than he'd bargained for.

"Nothing like a V-8 engine!" Carter declared and slapped the steering wheel. "Ain't that right, Travis?"

"Right," Travis managed, righting himself in his seat and wondering exactly what it was he was agreeing to. While touring Eagle River immediately after Katie's departure, the Carters had let him do the talking, but once inside their car and away from the town, Earl Carter had taken charge of the conversation. Travis had been trying to catch up ever since.

He'd been grateful when Sandra Carter had offered to ride in the back seat with their son, sure that his seat next to Earl would give him the perfect opportunity to observe and ask questions, but he'd been kept busy trying to answer them instead. And, while he was anxious to observe everything that went on inside the car as well as out, too much was going on at once for him to get a firm handle on anything.

"Lots of power," Carter continued. "This baby can outrun anything."

"It's certainly faster than a horse." The comment had everyone laughing, but Travis wasn't sure he got the joke. He was still trying to figure out exactly what made the car work. A key turned it on, pushing a pedal made it go, but why? Everywhere he looked there were buttons and knobs, but what they all did was a mystery. Yet one knob had turned on a thing of fascination. A flick of the wrist had made a box to the right of the steering wheel light up, and ever since sound had been bouncing around the interior of the car. Music, voices. Carter called it radio.

"Hancock's just up ahead," Carter said, bringing Travis's attention back to him. He cast the younger man a glance. "You got yourself a little lady waiting there?"

"Lady?" Travis repeated. "No, not exactly. I mean, she lives on a ranch nearby."

"Going to meet her later, that it?"

"Later," Travis agreed, but sooner came first and in no time the streets of the town called Hancock came into view, and Earl Carter was pulling the car over to a curb.

"Here we are," Carter announced and gestured to all that lay beyond the windshield.

Travis was already gawking out the window, staring at the buildings lining the streets, at the storefront windows and large signs, at the flashing lights and myriad of people. He swallowed tightly. This was his destination. This was where he'd wanted to go, but having arrived, it was difficult not to ask Earl Carter to turn the car around and take him back. Struggling against the surge of fear, Travis turned to extend his hand to Carter. He wasn't going to run. He had a job to finish. "Thank you for the ride."

"Glad I could help."

The man's grip was sure and warm while the metal handle that opened the door was stiff and cold. Travis tried to ignore the contrast as he stepped outside with a pounding heart, and waited while Sandra Carter moved from the back seat to the front. He closed the door for her once she was sitting again and bent to look inside. "Thanks again."

Earl Carter waved, Sandra smiled, and the car moved.

Travis stepped back to lift a hand in silent parting as they drove away, and fear once again threatened to overwhelm him. He was being left behind, deserted in the middle of a town he'd never heard of. That he'd wanted to come didn't in any way relieve the anxiety of finding himself alone in a time and place he knew little to nothing about.

Travis dropped his hand and stared in tight-fisted silence at the town around him. It was like none he'd ever seen. The buildings were big, constructed of metal and brick instead of logs and wood. The streets were smooth sheets of rock, not dirt or cobblestone, and huge street lamps lined the curbs. He tipped his head back to follow one of the poles up into the sky. In broad daylight none of the glass orbs was lit, but their size testified to their being bigger and better than the electric lighting he'd seen in Helena in 1882.

His gaze dropped back to the street. The lamps above him wouldn't just glow as those long ago had. These would shine brightly enough to rival the sun.

A loud roar suddenly came from his left, and Travis jumped back in alarm as a huge semitruck rumbled into view. With a hiss of brakes and a grinding of gears, the mammoth machine approached, and Travis beat a hasty retreat as the pavement beneath his feet trembled and the panes of glass behind him rattled. Coming up against the building wall, he stopped and watched with wide eyes and a racing heart as the truck rolled past. It was by far and away the biggest motorized vehicle he'd ever seen.

As the truck disappeared up the street, Travis lifted a trembling hand to wipe the sweat from his upper lip and glanced nervously up and down the walks. In Eagle River, while slipping in and out of his void in time, he'd seen many cars and trucks come and go, and he'd grown somewhat used to the change in transportation if not the noise. He frowned as he listened. In Hancock the hum of traffic was incessant, much louder than it had ever been in Eagle River, but he was the only one who seemed bothered by the constant roll of wheels and knock of engines. Everyone else he could see seemed oblivious to the sounds.

Fighting the anxiety urging him to run back to Eagle River and what sanctuary he could find there, Travis forced himself to focus on those sharing the roadside with him. He watched men and women walk and talk, saw them smile and gesture and found comfort in realizing that they, at least, hadn't changed with time. Their clothes might be different along with their hairstyles, but people were people whether they lived in 1883 or 1994, and they still had the same kind of jobs.

Across from him stood a barbershop. Next door was a hardware store. Grasping straws of the familiar,

Travis let his gaze continue to wander until he found two signs that had him stepping back toward the curb. One building promised to provide him a means to survive in the uncertain future he found himself in. The other offered a way to gain understanding and an ability to cope.

Travis unclenched and clenched his fists. Any doubts he'd had about why he'd come forward in time had vanished when he had greeted the Carters and they had responded in turn back in Eagle River. He was alive again because Katie Shannon needed him, and if he was going to help her, his fears of the unknown had to be put aside.

Unconsciously his hand rubbed his right hip. He longed for the comfort and security of his Colt, but time had ended the accepted practice of wearing and carrying firearms. He'd had to leave his six-gun back in Eagle River. That meant the only weapons he had were his wits, patience and determination. He gritted his teeth. Those would have to be enough.

Glancing once more up and down the street, Travis turned and began walking toward the store boasting a large sign that spelled out the word Antiques. That would be his first stop. He needed money to get a stake, modern currency to buy what he needed in the way of clothing and necessities, and once he had those he could move on to his second stop. The library. He had over one hundred years of reading to catch up on.

MILES AWAY, KATIE TURNED the Jeep onto the ranch road. Despite the need to hurry back to the ranch, she'd taken her time, dawdling when she should have been rushing home. But she couldn't regret delaying her return. She'd enjoyed and wanted to savor the time she'd spent in Eagle River, and a smile remained on her lips as she continued to think of the old ghost town and its acting sheriff, Travis McCord.

Her smile grew as she thought of him. What a strange man he was. Not once had he fallen out of character as he'd conducted the tour, talking as if he'd really lived back in 1883 and really known all the people he'd told her about. During the two hours she'd spent with him, he'd goofed up only once, and that had been at the cemetery with his namesake—if it was his namesake.

Katie bit her lip in silent speculation. Was Travis McCord his real name or only part of the role he played as caretaker for the old ghost town? She shrugged. Whatever the case might be, the modern-day Travis McCord didn't much like the late Travis. Her smile abruptly returned. After wondering for years what the enigmatic and legendary sheriff of Eagle River had looked like, her curiosity had finally been satisfied, and it was hard to imagine finding anyone who could better fit the bill of hero than the man presently holding the job. She sighed out loud. Straight and tall with dark hair, the current Travis McCord had the bluest eyes she'd ever seen!

The ranch buildings abruptly came into view, and Eagle River and its sheriff were temporarily forgotten. The homestead wasn't grand, but it was warm in winter, cool in summer and beautiful to her at any time. The ranch was home. It was where she belonged, and it caused her pain to realize she might lose all or part of it if she didn't come up with some solutions soon.

Pulling up before the rambling one-story house, she was surprised to see her stepfather's car out front and as surprised to see Mark Harrison coming down the steps. She jumped out of the Jeep to meet him at the bottom step.

"Mark, I hope you weren't waiting for me." She watched him smile in response to her greeting, but as always the warmth on his lips didn't reach the depths of his eyes. Katie suppressed a shiver and suddenly thought again of Travis McCord.

Mark Harrison was as tall and broad as Travis, but that was where the similarities ended. Travis had a genuine spontaneity and kindness about him. Her new foreman was cold in manner and expression. With his coal black hair and black eyes, she always felt he was looking down at her and not only because of her size. But he was a good foreman. At least, he had been so far.

Harrison's hand touched the brim of the Stetson he wore. "We were going to go over those figures for the cattle sale."

Katie grimaced. "I know. I'm sorry. I have them in the study, but I got held up. Trust me to make the right decision?"

He nodded. "You're the boss."

With another tip of the hat he was gone, walking away and across the yard toward the bunkhouse. Katie bit her lip as she watched him go. Mark Harrison never pressed her. He was quiet in his suggestions, but once he got a course of action in his head, he wasn't likely to alter it. He liked things done his way even if she didn't agree with him—or if the men didn't. Her frown deepened as she turned to go up the steps to the house. It worried her that the men hadn't taken to Mark. It was important they respect the foreman, as it was he who gave the orders.

With Bill Henry that had never been a worry. Everyone had liked and trusted Bill, and she had shared every question and problem about the ranch with him. When confronted by a mountain of debts on her mother's death, she hadn't hesitated to turn to him for help, and Bill hadn't hesitated to give it. He had been as shocked as she to see the ranch running in the red when there was no reason it should have been, but that hadn't stopped him from finding solutions to get the books back in the black again. Under his guidance the figures had rapidly begun falling back into place, but the accident had put her back on her own. She made all the decisions. The ranch was her sole responsibility, and sometimes the burden of it was nearly too heavy to bear.

The front door opened under her hand, and she walked in to meet her stepfather in the hall. "Simon." Moving forward, she accepted his warm hug. "I wasn't expecting you!"

"Disappointed?"

"Of course not." She smiled up into the warm brown of his eyes. A handsome man at the age of fifty-two, his dark hair was tinged with streaks of gray, but he kept himself in good physical condition and his dress was always immaculate.

He released her to motion to the front door. "Your foreman seemed a bit unhappy you weren't here."

"I lost track of time," Katie said, looping her arm with his to walk into the study off the hall. It had been her father's favorite room, and it was where she did all the book work for the ranch. "I was supposed to meet him here to go over the projected figures for the fall cattle sale, but I stopped by Eagle River and . . ." She shrugged.

Simon laughed. "You do love that old busted-up town."

Katie felt the need to justify her visit even though she knew Simon thought it best to leave the past behind. "It's part of my heritage. Steve Hunnicutt lived there, and today I met a new caretaker who knew a lot of the history of the town. I can't believe some of the stories he told! Makes me wonder if he made them up."

"Probably did. Anything to keep the tourists happy."

Katie tried not to let Simon's ready agreement dim the joy the tales had given her, but a frown came nevertheless when she stopped by the desk. Was it her imagination, or had some of the papers she'd left lying on it been moved? Surely Mark hadn't tried to go through the paperwork in her absence? Suddenly she was thankful she'd locked everything of importance in the desk before leaving the house earlier. "So what brings you out here? Some of my cooking?"

Simon laughed. "You did inherit your mother's gift with a frying pan, but I'm afraid this is just a short visit to say hello and to check on how things are going."

Katie felt her stomach sink. For all his good intentions, she wasn't ready for another of Simon's gentle lectures about giving up the ranch. "Everything's fine. I'm going to make it. I went over the figures last night. It's not as bad as all that."

Simon cocked an eyebrow at her.

"Trust me, will you? I'm not going to let the ranch fall to ruin yet."

"Going to tell the old man what you're planning?"

She shook her head. Simon meant well, but she couldn't confide in him as she had her real father, or even Bill. She loved Simon. He'd been good to her, but she'd never developed a rapport with him. Perhaps she had been too old when he had wed her mother. Or perhaps their likes and dislikes were too different. He didn't feel about the ranch the way she did, and he never would. "I'm going to surprise you."

"You always do. You're very resourceful. Just like your mother."

"It's the Hunnicutt pioneer spirit."

Simon grinned and looked at his watch. "I hate to run but..."

"I know. Business calls." She walked out of the study to the front porch with him. "What plans do you have for lunch tomorrow? I was thinking of going into town to pick up some odds and ends."

"If you come, give me a call. I can always make time for my girl." He kissed her cheek, winked and walked away to the big silver car that was part of the image he felt was important to his customers.

Katie's smile was warm as she watched him drive away, but it quickly faded when she turned back to the house. She wasn't *maybe* going to town in the morning. She was. To the bank. For things weren't really as bad as she'd thought. They were worse.

Returning to the study and the big oak desk, Katie sank into the worn leather chair behind it with a worried frown. She had no cash to pay debts or to operate the ranch. She'd depleted the accounts at the bank. The only thing left to do was to get a loan, and to do that she had to put the ranch up as collateral and pray the beef market held, the roundup went well and the winter wasn't bad. Any catastrophe could put her into bankruptcy and the ranch into the hands of a stranger.

YET SOMEHOW KATIE FELT optimistic as she drove to Eagle River two days later on Saturday morning. The bank had been willing to back her based on the reputation of her family and on the strength of the ranch's value, and the banker had been an old friend and classmate. She'd been embarrassed at first to learn she'd have to bare her soul—and her pocketbook—to an acquaintance, but it had been amazingly easy once the first hurdle had been taken.

She'd had to spend a few hours going over all her figures and filling out the necessary papers, but the final documents would be ready for her signature in less than a week. One sweep of the pen would give her a full line of credit. She'd have to go into debt for a while, but if the roundup went well, she'd be able to pay off the loan in no time with a little pinching.

Eagle River came into view as the Jeep rolled over the hill, and a smile burst across her face. She was really looking forward to showing Travis the ranch. With his love of history and knowledge of Steve and Molly Hunnicutt, she was sure he would like seeing what had become of the ranch those two pioneers had started.

She stopped the Jeep in front of the saloon and jumped out, pulling off her sunglasses as she hurried up the steps. She'd forgotten to ask Travis where to pick him up, but the saloon seemed the most logical spot, since that's where they'd met before. Yet when she got inside, Travis was nowhere to be seen.

Frowning against the sharp jab of disappointment, Katie walked to the bar. She had thought he'd be waiting and ready to go. Her frown deepened as she looked around the empty room. Had she misread his interest in seeing the ranch? She glanced at her watch. It wasn't ten yet. She was early. Smothering a sigh, she began to pace the floor. Just because she was anxious for the day to begin didn't mean he was. No doubt Travis would come once he saw the Jeep outside. She'd just have to be patient.

Humming to herself, she smiled as she remembered some of the wild tales he'd told her about the saloon. The miners and ranchers hadn't liked each other much even though the miners had depended on the ranchers for food. It seemed they were always accusing each other of being troublemakers when they were often both at fault. She glanced at her watch again. Ten o'clock. Her frown returned. Travis hadn't struck her as the kind of man to be late for an appointment.

She stopped to lean against the dusty bar. What if he'd been called away? Travis wouldn't have known how to reach her. Her teeth caught her lower lip. She should have given him her phone number. Still, she was in the book. If he'd had to leave, he could have called her.

Ten more minutes dragged past before she reluctantly turned to walk to the door. Her shoulders were bent and her steps heavy as she went. Yet she had no right to be disappointed. What did it matter that Travis McCord had stood her up? He was just a stranger. They meant nothing to each other. But she'd been so sure he'd be waiting and, stranger or not, she'd really wanted to see him again.

Part of it, she had to admit, was simple attraction. Travis McCord was all man. He had looks, charm and a male magnetism that made her skin tingle and her heart pound. Yet it was more than that. Ever since driving away and leaving him two days ago, Travis had been with her. Somehow he'd touched her in a way no one else ever had. With him she had felt . . . whole. It was as if, until she'd met him, a piece of her had been missing. Foolishly she'd thought he'd felt the same. But she'd been wrong. What she'd experienced had only been the love of a moment, the sharing of a past no one else but her father had ever really cared about.

She stepped out onto the porch and looked at the sagging timber of the falling buildings around her. Simon had been right. Travis had only been doing his job in escorting her around and humoring her questions. Or, worse, perhaps he hadn't even existed. What if Sheriff Travis McCord had only been a figment of her overactive imagination? As someone she had desperately needed and wanted to see, maybe he had only lived for her alone for a short space in time, and she'd never see him again.

Chapter Three

"I was beginning to think you were never coming out."

Katie gasped at the words and spun to see Travis leaning casually against the Jeep. He was dressed much the same as he had been when she'd first seen him. The only things missing were the tin star and the gun belt. The absence of the wide belt somehow managed to make him appear taller and his legs longer, and her heart leapt as the pure maleness of him hit her hard. But the rapid increase in her pulse was also motivated by joy. He had come! Leaping down the steps, she landed in front of him and was nearly overcome with the irresistible urge to hug him. She suppressed it by clasping her hands tightly behind her back. "You're late. I didn't think you were coming."

Travis pushed himself away from the Jeep, liking the way her eyes shone as she stared up at him. She was glad to see him, and he was shaken by how happy he was to see her. Never had anyone looked so good to him—and never had he been so glad to be able to look someone in the eye. The smile on his lips echoed hers, but the sudden yearning to take her in his arms had little to do with his intention of helping her. More, it had to do with helping himself. The struggle to keep his motives firmly in line was brief but intense. "Where I come from, it isn't polite to keep a lady waiting."

"Really?" Katie couldn't keep herself from staring up at him like some star-struck idiot. It didn't make any sense that a complete stranger could affect her the way he did, but with her blood heating under his gaze, her reaction couldn't be denied. She finally gestured to the Jeep. "You're ready to go?"

"If you are."

"Climb in."

Travis did and glanced around the compact little vehicle as soon as he was seated. He was fast getting used to the current mode of transportation, but he still wasn't sure if he preferred it over a horse. The modern machinery could get someone somewhere faster than a horse, but the feeling just wasn't the same.

Katie stepped inside and put on her sunglasses. "Hope you don't mind women drivers."

"Are they worse than men?"

She burst out laughing. "That's the rumor." She started the Jeep and shifted into gear for a smooth start. "So, did you have any more visitors since I came?"

"I did."

"Nice, I hope?"

"Very. They gave me a ride to town."

"To Hancock? Don't you have your own car?"

"I don't even have a horse."

Katie laughed again, not sure if he was pulling her leg or not. "What did you do in town?"

"Read a lot." And walked a lot. He didn't want to remember all the walking and gawking he'd done since he'd seen her last, but Hancock had been a place of amazement with its paved roads, neon signs, traffic and pedestrians.

After the Carters had left him, he'd begun searching for a place to sell the old coins he'd been carrying before going about buying himself some new clothes—at exorbitant prices—and a few other necessities. Time hadn't permitted him to get to the library before it closed. He'd had to wait until the next day, but his research into the times had begun in a café that remained open all night. Drinking coffee and poring over magazines and newspapers, he'd read the hours away, trying to comprehend the current state of the world while waiting for the library to reopen.

Friday morning he was through the library doors as soon as they were unlocked, and he'd stayed the day, not leaving until after nightfall when most of the citizens were gone and the streets were nearly deserted. He'd nearly panicked when he could find no way to return to Eagle River where he was to meet Katie in the morning, but with quite a bit of the current paper money left after his shopping expeditions, he'd been able to convince a young boy with a battered pickup truck to drive him back.

"You were at the library?" Katie asked. And at his nod, "Miss Preston won't bother you at all as long as you don't make any noise."

Travis frowned. "Skinny woman with a long nose?"

"That's the one."

"She was a big help. Gave me all the books I wanted. Even let me stay late."

Katie caught his grin and grimaced. With a smile like that, Travis McCord could probably have asked to stay the night, and Lois Preston would have let him. "What were you reading about?"

"Everything that's happened over the last hundred years or so."

Katie laughed. "You really do like your history, don't you?"

"I had a lot to catch up on." At her puzzled frown, he just grinned. Trying to lie was too complicated, and trying to explain would make him sound like a lunatic. He had to gain Katie's confidence, convince her that he could help her, before he tried to justify his presence in her life. Not that he understood it too well himself.

"Being out here alone would tend to make you feel cut off from everything," she finally conceded and glanced at him as the Jeep bounced its way over the dirt road and left a billowing cloud of dust in their wake. "Does your family live near here?"

"I don't have any family. My father died when I was fifteen and my mother when I was twenty."

"I'm sorry. No brothers or sisters?"

"Nope."

"Do you mind being alone?"

"I'm not alone anymore."

The warmth of the gaze that caught hers had heat rushing into her cheeks, but before she could think of anything to say, he spoke again.

"You were close to your mother."

"Yes, and my father. We always spent a lot of time together."

"It must have been hard when your father died."

She nodded. "For my mother especially, I think." As a young girl, a teenager full of herself and consumed by her own grief, it had taken time for her to realize that she wasn't the only one in pain. Their grief had drawn them together. "My parents were very close. My mother missed my dad."

"And she married again?"

"A few years later."

"What about your stepfather? You said he didn't live on the ranch any more?"

"Simon belongs in and to the city."

"Not everyone likes the isolation of a ranch," Travis offered.

"And not everyone likes cattle." She laughed as she turned onto the county highway. "Simon can't ride very well, much less rope a calf."

"Can you?"

"Of course. This boss lady makes sure she's part of every roundup, though I don't imagine it's the same as it was back when Steve Hunnicutt was alive."

Travis frowned. "Why not?"

Katie gave him a baffled frown. "Because Steve Hunnicutt didn't have trucks and helicopters."

"Helicopters?" Travis asked, searching through his recently acquired memory for some insight as to what they could be.

"The ranch doesn't own one, but my neighbors do. Every year Ed comes down to help us flush the cattle out of the forest. We never get all of them, but we do pretty good," she explained. "The rest we do like they did a hundred years ago—on horseback. With the mountains and trees, the trucks just can't get in deep enough."

Still trying to define helicopter, Travis grasped at understanding what he could. "Your neighbor and you do a joint roundup?"

"It's easiest if we work together. Ed starts from one end, and we from the other. By the time we meet somewhere in the middle, most of the strays are sorted out, and all that's left is the branding and head count."

Travis nodded. He hadn't always been a sheriff, and he remembered well the long hours in the saddle and the endless days it had taken to gather the herd before starting the drive to the railheads.

"It still takes a lot of time to get the job done, but my great-great-grandfather would be pleased to know even though the spread is bigger now and carries more cattle, we can still finish in less time than he could— thanks to the trucks and other modern engineering wonders." She caught Travis frowning and asked, "Ever try to herd a steer on a snowmobile?"

"Snowmobile?" he repeated, too well aware that he was out of his depth. He'd tried to read everything he could about ranching as well as history at the library, but obviously he'd missed a few details.

"Maybe I should ask if you ever herded any cattle."

"I wasn't always the sheriff of Eagle River," he objected, pride coming to his rescue. "I've put a rope on a steer more than a few times."

Katie grinned at him, wondering if she should doubt the truth of his statement—and some of the other things he'd told her since they'd met. But she preferred to believe him. "Okay, Sheriff, no insult intended. Reading books and preserving history are just as important as punching cattle. Whenever anyone sneered at any city slicker, my father always said all men had their places and their own jobs to do."

"I think I like your father."

Katie smiled. "Everyone did."

She turned onto the road leading to the ranch, and Travis searched the land around him for familiar landmarks. He found some and noted others that had come to pass over the years. He was also fascinated by the poles and wires strung along the road. Not telegraph anymore. Rather, it was telephone. Voice communication, one-on-one, not by printed word. "I always liked to read," he said suddenly, feeling the need to justify his bookwormish image to Katie when it seemed to somehow separate them from each other. "Got it from my mother."

"She liked to read?"

"She was a teacher."

"And she taught you?"

"We weren't always by a school."

Katie frowned. "I don't understand."

"We traveled a lot." Travis grinned. "My father could never stand to stay in one spot long."

Katie felt a wave of sympathy for the boy Travis who must have been uprooted time and again. "It must have been hard for you. What did he do?"

"Bookkeeper. At least, during the day." And, at her prompting look, he added, "He spent a lot of time with a deck of cards."

"Cards? I've heard of people going bonkers on the lottery or betting on the ponies, but I didn't think cards were that popular anymore. Not for gambling, anyway."

"He always managed to find a game," Travis explained and made mental notes to look up *helicopter*, *snowmobile* and *lottery* when next he got to the library. He still had a lot to learn.

Katie slowed the Jeep to turn through the gates and onto the ranch. "Welcome to the Double S."

"Not the Bar H?"

She grinned. "My mom changed it for my dad when they got married. I don't think he ever got used to the idea. He wanted to change it back but at the same time didn't want to hurt my mother's feelings."

Travis nodded but said nothing, sitting back in the seat instead to stare through the windshield. Suddenly he was anxious to see the ranch, to see what Steve had done with it. Somehow the homestead seemed farther east than he remembered, but it was confusing following roads that turned every which way rather than going straight across the land to the house.

Abruptly Katie slowed to a halt on a slight rise in the road and silently got out to lead the way to the front of the Jeep.

Travis followed, joining her there to stare down at the buildings that made up the Double S. Gone was the homestead he remembered. It had been replaced by the impressive spread of neatly painted structures below him. To the far left sat the ranch house. A low building with simple lines and a classic, homey sprawl, it had lots of windows and was backed by the slope of the land that led to distant mountains. Its front door overlooked the other buildings and ranch yard, and from its porch the rich earth that stretched out to the meadows and plains beyond could be seen.

He didn't know and recognize all the structures for what they were, but the barn and surrounding corrals were set in familiar lines, as was the bunkhouse—a fancier one than he'd ever seen. Various types of vehicles—trucks and Jeeps mostly—were parked around the yard or could be seen through open doors with other ranch equipment. He supposed some of them belonged to the ranch and others to the ranch hands, since a cowboy didn't ride a horse all the time anymore.

"Like it?"

Travis nodded sharply but didn't look at Katie. He was too overwhelmed by the size and splendor of what had come from his friend's efforts, and the pride he felt brought moisture to his eyes. "It's not where the original homestead sat."

"No, this site was chosen in the early 1900s by Billy. After his father died and he was on his own, he moved the house here when he married."

"Made a place for himself and his bride," Travis said, the tightness in his chest growing as he remembered the little boy with the mop of blond hair, a ton of freckles and an endless stream of questions. "He did good."

Puzzled by the emotion in his voice, Katie watched Travis as he stared out at the ranch, but his expression was hard to see beneath the brim of his hat. "I can take you out to the old homestead if you'd like. We still use it, especially during roundup. We camp there instead of coming all the way back here. It saves time."

Travis nodded and turned to meet the questions in her eyes. "I'd like that, but right now I think I'd like to see more of what Billy did."

Reassured by his steady gaze, Katie smiled and moved back to the Jeep. "I'm glad you like it. It's not as big and grand as some, but it's home."

He climbed into the Jeep beside her, and his eyes caught hers. "Home's important."

Suddenly lost in the warmth of his stare, Katie felt her heart leap into her throat. During the drive she'd forgotten how attractive Travis McCord was. Not being able to watch him as they'd talked, she hadn't been conscious of the width of his shoulders, the strong cut of his jaw or the all-consuming blue of his eyes.

Unprepared for and confused by the strength of her feelings, she quickly pulled away from his gaze and turned the key in the ignition to start the Jeep once more. If her hands were shaking just a little, she hoped he didn't notice, but then the trembling of her fingers was slight compared to the quaking of her heart. The eruption of sexual attraction was something she hadn't expected, but should have. Travis was a good-looking man, and she was, after all, only human.

Thankfully, upon reaching the yard, Travis's attention was quickly diverted when she introduced him to a few of her ranch hands, and afterward it became next to impossible to respond to her body's reactions to him when he kept making her use her mind. If she'd asked him a lot of questions while he'd shown her around Eagle River, Travis asked her dozens more. He wanted to know everything.

The only break she got was during lunch. When the men of the ranch paused to eat, she took Travis to join them, and he began putting questions to them instead of her. Amazed at his endless quest for knowledge, she sat and watched him pry answers out of even the quietest ranch hand, but what was more incredible was the men's reaction to his open curiosity. Normally a few questions from a stranger were more than plenty, but Travis had a way of getting around the stigma of stranger and made the men respond to him.

Studying him over coffee, Katie thought perhaps it was that Travis obviously knew something about ranching. He didn't ask dumb questions, and his interest in the answers was genuine, not just a facade. He really wanted to know what the men had to say, and they sensed it. Travis gave them respect for what and who they were, and he offered them simple justification for what could have been seen as rudeness.

"It's been a while since I've worked at a ranch."

With those few words he earned acceptance and answers, and he absorbed everything he heard like a sponge. But that was Travis's intent. He had to learn. He had to know all he could if he was to help Katie.

The more time he spent with her, the more he was sure that was what he had and wanted to do. She was not only an attractive woman but an intelligent one. She knew the ranch, she knew what it took to make it run, and she was doing her best to make it work—and so were her men. It pleased him to see the easy camaraderie she shared with her hired hands and to note that she joined them for a meal without any trace of self-consciousness or doubt. The simple action spoke volumes about how much both the ranch and the men meant to her, and their easy acceptance of her presence at their dinner table told him that the feeling was mutual.

After lunch Travis trailed after some of the men with Katie tagging along. All the new equipment and modern machinery both fascinated and frightened him. It was obvious the inventions had made many aspects of ranch work easier, but having no idea how to operate any of them, he was glad to see the daily chores, at least, were basically the same. Harness still broke, fences still needed mending, horses needed to be broken and stock had to be fed and cared for.

Alone with Katie again in one of the outbuildings, Travis ran a cautious hand over a mean-looking piece of machinery. "You harvest hay with this?"

"Yes."

"You drive it?"

She grinned and nodded as he pushed the hat back on his head to stare at the mower. "What's wrong, McCord, never drive a tractor?"

He shook his head and stepped back. "Driving a six-horse team was as complicated as my skills got when I was ranching."

She grabbed his arm and pulled him toward the door. "Why don't I believe you?"

"You should."

Stepping out into the sunlight, Katie turned to retort further but was struck silent by the sincere honesty etched across his face and the earnest plea in his eyes.

"I'll never lie to you, Katie."

Caught again in the warmth of his gaze, her heart jumped, and dizzying waves of sensation had her head spinning.

Travis felt the impact, too. The breath caught in his chest, and desire flooded his blood. He put out a hand toward her.

"Miss Shannon?"

Startled, Katie jumped in surprise and turned to find Mark Harrison approaching. A guilty flush stained her cheeks. One more second and she would have been caught necking in the middle of the ranch yard. "Mark. Back from town?"

"Yes. The men told me you were showing someone around. They thought he might be a new ranch hand."

"No," Katie told him and felt a sharp pang of regret. "Travis is only visiting." She gestured from one man to the other. "Mark Harrison, this is Travis McCord. Travis, this is Mark Harrison, my foreman."

Travis watched Harrison's mouth curve, but his eyes stayed cool. Dead. "Pleasure," Travis said politely and accepted a firm handshake with one of his own. The Double S foreman was dark in coloring and nature. His greeting and expression held no warmth, only a hint of resentment.

"From the area?" Harrison asked, his gaze quick to drop and scrutinize. The man before him was tall and strong, the physique gained through some type of manual labor—or an expensive health club.

"Yup. Last job was as the sheriff of Eagle River."

A bubble of laughter came from Katie, but she noted her foreman didn't so much as quirk an eyebrow. He just frowned, and Travis noted the lack of response, too. No sense of humor. Travis decided he didn't like Mark Harrison.

"I'll leave you alone, then." Harrison dismissed them both with a polite tip of his hat.

Katie bit her lip as she watched her foreman go, not having missed the derisive tone or the significant look she'd received. The introduction had wasted his time. Mark wasn't interested in meeting anyone except somebody willing and able to help with the ranch. And, he was still waiting to talk to her about the coming roundup. He wanted to know what to prepare for, how much stock to sell, how much to keep, how much money she didn't have....

"Know him long?"

Her gaze came back to Travis. "No, he only came to the ranch after Bill died. Mark was recommended."

"Seems a bit young to be foreman."

Katie smiled up at him. "No younger than you."

Travis frowned. All the foremen he'd ever known had been older and more experienced, having worked at a spread for years before being given a position of authority. "I guess times have changed."

Katie laughed and rolled her eyes. "Will you stop talking as if you're still sheriff of Eagle River? This is 1994 not 1883." And before he could respond, she turned to the closest corral. "Come on, it's getting late, and I want you to see the old homestead where Steve Hunnicutt used to live." She turned to walk backward. "You can ride a horse?"

"That's one thing I'm very good at," Travis assured her with a quick grin.

"Such modesty."

"You just let me pick my own horse."

And he did. He chose a sorrel, top-quality stock with white stockings and long legs and lots of bottom, and Travis rode the mustang as if he'd been in the saddle for most of his life.

"You always surprise me," Katie told him as she followed him out of the ranch yard. Even one of the other hands had stopped to comment on Travis's eye for a good horse. "I never know what to expect from you next."

"How so?"

"You talk as if you know nothing about modern ranching yet you know about cattle and horses and the basics of making a ranch run."

"I told you I used to punch cattle."

"But on a ranch with no tractors or mowers?"

"We did everything by hand," he told her, avoiding her eyes as their horses carried them across the rolling Montana plains. It felt good to be in the saddle again. Good to be *alive* again, and he didn't want to ruin the enjoyment of the moment by trying to convince Katie of who he was. She'd never believe him. Not without proof, and he had none. "It was a small spread."

"Where?"

"In South Dakota some years back."

"And you decided you'd rather look after a ghost town than ranch?"

"Not exactly. A lot of things have happened in between then and now."

"Like what?"

He turned in the saddle to look at her. She rode naturally, easily, and she, too, had put on a Stetson to ride the range. It shaded her face, but even if he couldn't see the curiosity in her eyes, he could feel it. "I thought this was my day to ask all the questions?"

Katie blanched immediately. "I'm sorry. I didn't mean to be rude. I just want—"

"To know more about the sheriff of Eagle River."

The smile he gave her would have buckled her knees if she'd been standing, but she managed to nod. "You're different from anyone I've ever met," she told him, speaking without thinking.

"So are you." Their eyes locked, and once again Travis felt the pull of her as a woman warming his insides. It wasn't something he'd expected or wanted. Upon meeting her, he'd resolved to give Katie Shannon nothing more than friendship, but his body was sending him a different signal.

Her eyes dropped from his as a flush of color crept up her neck, and silently he cursed himself. He'd come to help Katie. That was what he'd been sent for. He was sure of it. Emotions couldn't get in the way. Besides, he was a man from the 1800s sent to the 1900s. What could he offer her beyond his protection when he didn't know if, when he'd accomplished what needed to be done, he'd be able to stay? Would his helping her release him to go to the grave he'd been meant to lie in years ago?

"I was born in Abilene," he said suddenly, wanting to share what he could of himself without losing her confidence. "Spent most of my life in one cow town or another. My father always found work in the local bank and my mother would teach." Travis grinned. "But my father loved cards more than banking."

"It must have been hard on your mother," Katie sympathized, thinking Travis must have had a hard life with his mother struggling to make ends meet while his father spent all the money on gambling.

"No, she took it well." At Katie's puzzled look, he said hastily, "My father didn't lose that much. He just liked to play. He liked to be where there was a lot of action. People coming and going."

"Oh."

Travis smiled. He didn't think Katie could understand thinking in modern terms. When his father had lived, the entire state of Kansas had been pulsing with the life given it by cattle drives and cowboys. Travis had grown up watching the herds coming in until his father had dragged him and his mother out to Nevada and the silver and gold strikes. Francis McCord hadn't wanted to dig for buried treasure. He'd only wanted to see what was brought out of the mines. "We eventually ended up in Nevada. My father worked for one of the mining companies."

"He must have liked that if the company was near Las Vegas."

Travis frowned. Las Vegas. There had been an army fort there for a while, Fort Baker, but mostly it had been a gateway to California. Obviously that had changed. "He liked anything that brought him close to a deck of cards."

"You said he died when you were fifteen?"

"Yes, when we were in Virginia City. My mother and I moved to San Francisco after he was gone, and she stayed there when I went out on my own." He gestured to the land ahead of them. "How far is it to the homestead?"

Katie accepted the change in subject with satisfaction. She still didn't understand all she wanted to about Travis McCord or his background, but some of her questions had been answered. "Actually, it's quite a way. It'll take us a couple hours to get there. We probably should have driven out. By the time we get there and back, it's going to be late, and you haven't even seen the house yet."

"Then why don't we go faster?"

Loping across the meadows under an early-afternoon sun, they alternately raced or walked over hills and through streams. They saw plenty of cattle and a circling hawk, and viewed the last of the spring flowers. Summer had arrived on the back of a warm wind.

By the time they reached the rise over which the old home of Steve Hunnicutt lay, the flanks of their horses were marked by sweat and Katie's cheeks were flushed with the excitement of a wild ride. She laughed as Travis stopped his horse beside hers. "It's been a long time since I've run like that." She reached down to pat her horse's neck.

"Why?"

She shrugged but refused to let any shadows dim the sunshine of the day. "Problems with the ranch have been taking up a lot of my time."

Travis noted the way her eyes once again avoided his, and his jaw clenched. How much trouble was the ranch in? "It'll all work out."

Her gaze met his once more, and she quickly grasped at the ray of hope he offered. When she was with him, somehow she really believed everything would be all right. "Yes, it will." She pointed ahead. "The homestead is just over this rise. It's changed some since it was built, but the house and barn are still pretty much the way they were." She started her horse forward again, and Travis eagerly followed until the buildings came into view.

Confronted with reality, he stopped to stare at the ranch yard spread out before him, and the truth hit him hard. The homestead he remembered was no more. It was gone. Really gone. And, his friends were dead. He followed Katie slowly, desperately searching for something of the familiar amidst the new and finding it when he looked in the right places. The worn rails Steve had used to make the corral were gone, but the enclosure remained where it had once stood. The chicken coop was missing, as was the storage shed, but the barn was still up—due to many repairs.

Stopping in front of the house, Katie slid from her horse to tie the reins to a hitching rail. "We can go right in. There's no one here now." She disappeared inside, but again, Travis was slow to follow.

Stepping from the saddle, he had to battle memories that threatened to overwhelm him. In his mind's eye he could see Steve waving to him from the barn, Molly hanging up the wash and Billy racing across the yard with his dog. For Katie the Hunnicutts had died long ago, but for him, they had been alive only yesterday. He swallowed tightly against the pain of loss and stepped into the house.

Pausing in the doorway, he stood still as his eyes adjusted to the change in lighting. Outside the sun was shining, but inside shadows abounded, and in them Travis saw the past. Walking hesitantly forward, he glanced down at the floor and remembered how he had helped Steve put the first boards in. The house had been built with a dirt floor, but Molly had wanted that changed as soon as possible.

His eyes searched the big room where he had often shared a meal with his friends. It had changed. The fireplace was the same, but the curtains on the windows were different. The bright yellow ones Molly had sewn by hand were gone, and the old rocking chair and handmade table had been replaced as well. Sorrow touched him as he looked around for what had been. The home he'd known had become just a building, an impersonal place men came to rest after a long day's work.

"The bedrooms are through those two doors," Katie commented, unaware of the loud pounding of Travis's heart. "There are bunk beds for the men to use, and the kitchen's over here." She grinned. "They kept the potbellied stove. It still works." She moved to stand before the big fireplace in the middle of the main room. "I always loved this. I bet the fires they built here came in handy on those cold winter nights."

"They did."

Katie frowned as she turned to look at him but didn't speak as he abruptly turned to stride outside. She followed and watched him restlessly pace the yard, believing she understood some of what he was feeling. "It's like Eagle River, isn't it?" she told him. "When it's quiet and the mood's just right, you can almost feel their presence."

Travis turned from studying the barn to stare at her. All he saw was death. The destruction of everything he'd loved. She saw, and continued to feel life. "Steve and Molly?"

She smiled as she felt his eyes on her, confident he knew what she meant. "They were happy here. I can feel it."

He walked slowly to her, the tension in his chest suddenly easing. For a moment he'd felt totally alone. Lost. Abandoned. But he wasn't by himself. He had Katie. "So can I."

Tears unexpectedly burned her eyes at his expression of understanding, and she looked down at her booted feet. "Do you want to stay awhile longer?"

Travis searched the ranch yard he had once known so well. He wasn't dreaming. The past was past, and the future was present. "No, we can go back. I've seen enough." More than enough. Walking with Katie to the horses, he felt overwhelmed by the changes time had made in his life. Everything he'd known was lost.

"Are you all right?" Katie asked, reaching out to take his hand. He seemed sad again, alone as he had been when she'd first seen him.

Travis struggled to pull himself out of the past, but couldn't. "I miss them."

"Steve and Molly?" She followed his gaze back to the homestead. She knew what it was like to be attached to what was gone, what had been. Her parents were gone, her life as she'd known it was over. She incorrectly assumed that as a man who loved what had been, Travis longed, as she did, for the past to live again. "But they're not gone. Not as long as we remember them."

Travis recognized her pain even as she recognized his, and his fingers tightened over hers. "I'll never forget."

She smiled up at him. "Neither will I."

By the time they got back to the ranch yard, the sun was setting, and the western horizon was streaked with red and orange ribbons of fading light.

"We can leave the horses by the corral," Katie told him as they dismounted. "I'll rub them down when I get back from taking you to Eagle River."

"I can do it."

Katie shook her head, sad to know Travis had to go but at the same time anxious that he be on his way so the parting could be over with and she could get back to the matters at hand. Her day with him had been one of the best she'd had in a long time, but the happiness he brought her was fleeting. "I like working with the horses."

"Me, too."

She turned determinedly away from his warmth and began walking toward the Jeep but stopped when she realized he wasn't following. With a frown she looked back to find him watching her. "Is something wrong?"

"I don't want to go."

The shadows were long in the yard and in her heart as she stood with him in the fading light of day. When would she see Travis again? Would she see him again? She didn't need the complication of a man in her life. She had enough problems already. "I'm glad you had a good time." But he still didn't move.

Travis gestured toward the bunkhouse. "Your foreman seemed to think I could fill an empty bed over there. You need an extra hand?"

Katie's mouth fell open in disbelief. "Are you asking me for a job?"

"Is that out of the question?"

"I—I . . ." She stammered for words as hope began to build. It shouldn't be so important that Travis stay. It couldn't mean that much. She'd only known him for a few days, been with him only a few hours, but when she was with him, everything was different. She felt hopeful. Happy. She believed everything was all right. "But what about your job in Eagle River?"

"I turned my badge in last night."

"You quit?"

He nodded.

"I don't know what to say."

"Say yes. Otherwise I won't have any place to sleep tonight." And if she didn't let him stay on the ranch, how could he help her? "I know I'm a little low on experience when it comes to some of the chores at the ranch, but I can learn."

"You don't even want to know how much I pay?"

"Can't be any worse than what I was getting," he grinned.

She laughed and abruptly twirled in a circle. "All right. You're hired, but we'll have to go to Eagle River to get your things."

"No, we don't. Everything's already in the Jeep."

She stared at him in surprise before spinning to look at the Jeep. She hadn't noticed anything different in its back, but then, she hadn't looked either. When she'd picked Travis up, she'd had eyes only for him. Turning around again to cast him a narrowed stare, her hands settled on her hips as she faced him once more. "That sure of yourself, were you?"

Travis gave her a smile that made her knees shake. "My friend Steve always told me I had a way with the ladies."

Chapter Four

Travis leaned forward to stare into the mirror and ran a hand across the whiskers on his jaw. Standing bare chested at one of the sinks in the bunkhouse after finishing his shower, he wore only jeans and boots. Fortunately, the ready jets of water and their handles were something he'd easily mastered and come swiftly to enjoy. But the modern-day razor...

He grimaced at the nicks he could still see on his neck and face. The new double-bladed, short-handled tools men used to shave with in 1994 weren't what he was used to. He sighed. But, they were all he had. He straightened and reached for the can of shaving cream and his new blade.

"McCord, I can't stand it. If you're going to shave again, use mine," Bob Casey, another ranch hand, protested from where he stood a few feet down the mirror from Travis. "Watching you butcher yourself day after day is more than a grown man can bear."

The objection brought a winning grin to Travis's face, an easy expression of good humor that had quickly won the confidence and friendship of the other Double S men. Thankfully, over the past week Katie hadn't interfered with him finding his place amongst the others working on the ranch. She'd left him to do that on his own, and Travis felt he'd done well enough. The only man he couldn't quite see eye to eye with was Mark Harrison, but he wasn't alone in that. Not many of the hands got along well with the ranch foreman. "I'm used to a straight razor."

"Forget that. Take this."

Travis automatically accepted the small contraption shoved into his hand. "But Bob—"

"No buts, McCord. I can't stand the sight of blood." Bob gestured to the electric razor. "The batteries are charged up. You shouldn't need the cord."

"Batteries?" Travis repeated.

"You know, the things that make the radio go when it's not plugged in." Bob, a man of thirty with a craggy face and thick mop of brown hair, replied with a grin and clapped Travis on the back. "You can put it on my bunk when you're done." With a wave Bob was gone, leaving Travis alone in the bathroom with a machine he didn't have the slightest idea how to use.

Travis brought the razor up to eye level to examine it. He'd seen Bob use it. He'd seen a couple of the hands use machines like it. The problem was he couldn't figure out how the razors worked. No soap and lather, just a flick of a switch and the job was done. The batteries that made it go had to be like electricity, a true marvel that certainly seemed to make life easier. Lights without candles, washing machines without scrub boards, radios instead of newspapers, refrigerators for cold food—and ice cubes all year round. But shaving?

He ran a finger over the metal screen that covered the blades and, taking a cautious look around the room to make sure he was alone, flicked the switch.

The razor jumped to life, buzzing and shaking with such intensity he almost dropped it, but Travis held on, trying to squeeze the razor into submission. His harsh grip had no impact on the instrument, but at least the vibrations that raced all the way up his arm didn't worsen.

Swallowing his misgivings, he cautiously put the razor to his face. It hit with an unexpected bite, and he jerked back. Scowling at the razor, Travis leaned forward for another try, watching closely in the mirror as he ran the blades over his cheek. To his astonishment, his whiskers actually disappeared. He grinned. It worked!

Running the razor over the planes of his face again and again, shaving took a good deal longer than normal, but it was hard not to keep playing with yet another wonder of the future. Still, time was wasting, and reluctantly Travis turned off the buzzing blades and left the washroom for Bob's bunk, where he left the razor. Walking back toward his own bunk, he raised a hand to run it across his jaw. Next time he went to town he'd have to see about getting one of the electric shavers for himself.

Abruptly, the phone rang as he passed it. Travis quickly looked around for someone to answer it, but he was the only one in sight. Hesitantly he reached for the instrument and picked it up. He'd seen the men use it but had never actually tried it himself except once when no one had been around. The only thing he'd heard had been a loud buzz.

"Bunkhouse," he said, repeating the words others had used when answering the phone, but he was uneasy as he held the instrument in his hand. Yet no buzz greeted him as before. Instead Katie's voice suddenly came through loud and clear.

"Travis? It's Katie."

He grinned. Telephones were definitely better than a telegraph! "I know. I can tell."

"Probably because I'm about the only woman around except for Helen," the answer came back.

"She's a good cook," Travis responded, taking the phone away from his ear to stare at it. It was amazing how close Katie sounded. She could have been standing right next to him!

"I'm glad you approve. She's my last foreman's wife, and she's been fixing the food for the ranch for years."

"I know that, too." He'd learned a lot of things over the past week about the people on the ranch, and Helen Henry had been one source of information. An older woman with a son working on the ranch and a daughter away in college, she had stayed on after her husband's death to continue working on the ranch as she had for years. "She likes you."

Katie flushed as she stood in the kitchen of the ranch house. "I like her, too. She's a good friend." When he didn't speak again, she added, "Are you ready to go to Tyler's place?"

Travis nodded even though she couldn't see. When they'd met in the barn a day before, he'd asked her if she could take him to Tyler Fenton's place on his day off. Her eyes had lit with pleasure at his request, and the shy smile that had followed had knocked his equilibrium off center. "I'll meet you outside in five minutes."

"Okay."

Travis hung up, and grinned at the phone just as Gus Mitchum, one of the other men, came by. "Amazing," he told the older hand, who had gray in his hair but life in his step.

Gus grinned back and shook his head. Travis McCord had become a ready source of entertainment with his simple pleasure at things everyone else had long since come to take for granted, but then not everyone had worked on a big spread with a lot of the conveniences. "Better than shouting."

One of the other younger hands, Mike Gardine, came on behind Gus and punched Travis in the shoulder with his fist. "You are weird, McCord."

Not at all insulted and still grinning, Travis moved away from the phone and back to his cubicle. The bunkhouse hadn't been quite what he'd expected when he'd arrived. Used to a one-room structure piled with bunk beds, he'd been pleasantly surprised to find that the privacy of the men had come to be taken into consideration.

The bunkhouse still had a community room where the men gathered and talked, but the sleeping areas had been sectioned off into cubicles. There were even a few small rooms for the hands with seniority. Travis had found a cubicle by himself and was probably better off for it with the way his curiosity always had him playing with some new invention that had come his way.

Tossing the towel he'd had over his shoulder onto his bed, he shrugged into a shirt as he returned to the bathroom. What with electricity and indoor plumbing, he was quickly growing used to modern-day living. In just a few days he'd come to wonder how he'd ever survived without all the conveniences the future had wrought.

Satisfied with his appearance in a long-sleeved cotton shirt and blue jeans, he went back to his bunk. It still seemed odd not to wear his Colt all the time, but he was getting used to leaving the gun in the bottom of a drawer below some extra clothes. He grabbed his Stetson and headed for the door. He didn't want to keep Katie waiting.

Stepping outside into the warm Montana sunshine, Travis put on his hat and started walking to where he knew the Jeep was parked. The ranch yard was empty of people. It was Sunday, and it was early. Almost every man had off except for those whose turn it was to feed the animals in the barn and do some miscellaneous chores. A car door slammed, and Travis turned to see Mark Harrison starting up his bright red pickup truck. Travis frowned. He'd had a hard time dealing with the Double S foreman. Harrison was not easy to like or work for and had taken peculiar pleasure in trying to single him out for some of the more laborious chores around the ranch.

As the new hand, Travis had expected to be given the least glamorous and dirtiest jobs. It was part of a standard ranch routine he'd experienced before, but Mark Harrison put his teeth on edge. He didn't like the way the man gave orders, the way he treated the other hands, or the way he talked to Katie. She was a small woman, but her size had nothing to do with the way Harrison appeared to stand over her. Yet she held her own. Harrison didn't always get his way. Still, it was just a good thing, as foreman, he had his own house away from the rest of the men. Had he lived in the bunkhouse, the atmosphere might have gotten downright unpleasant once in a while—if not violent.

The red pickup disappeared up the road, and Travis faced forward again to see Katie coming down the porch steps toward the Jeep, and his heart skipped a beat. She looked soft and fresh and filled out the T-shirt and jeans she wore in pleasing style. Outhouses and cold baths weren't the only things he didn't miss. He was beginning to believe gingham dresses were best left in the past, too.

Katie stopped by the Jeep and smiled at Travis's approach, feeling suddenly shy as he came to a halt in front of her and put his fingers to his hat in polite greeting. He was so tall and good-looking she wanted to pinch herself whenever she saw him to make sure she wasn't dreaming. And, she couldn't get over the rightness of his presence on the ranch. It was as if he belonged. Everyone had certainly accepted him easily enough. At least, everyone except her foreman. Mark hadn't been happy with her hiring someone without consulting him.

"References," he'd told her. "We should have gotten references from other ranches where he's worked."

"His last job wasn't on a ranch—"

"Exactly. How do we know he's not just talking when he says he knows how to punch cattle?"

The conversation had gone on for some time before her foreman had stomped off none too happy, and it hadn't been the last one she'd had with him about Travis. Mark seemed determined to discredit Travis and had been trying at every opportunity to point out his shortcomings. But his efforts were based on nothing concrete except where it concerned the use of ranch equipment. Travis didn't know how to work the machinery. Anything with a motor was beyond him, but he had been honest about his ignorance at the start and that had been her defense of him to Mark.

But to insure her better judgment wasn't being influenced by her attraction to Travis, she'd made certain of his knowledge by bringing casual comments into conversations with the other men when he wasn't around. They all seemed to like Travis. He was the butt of many a good ribbing because he seemed to be approaching all the ranch tasks with an 1800s perspective, but that was blamed on his being a historian and on "reading more than doing." And he took it all with good grace and a tolerant smile. Yet he was a quick learner. If he made a mistake once, it didn't happen again.

All in all, she couldn't believe she'd been wrong to hire Travis even though he made her heart pound and her head spin whenever he smiled at her. It probably wasn't wise to feel that way considering he was her employee, but as she found herself enveloped in the warmth of his gaze, it was impossible to regret the way she felt. "Morning."

"Morning." He looped his fingers in the belt around his waist as he stared down at her. It was the only way he could resist reaching out to brush his fingertips over the warm expanse of skin exposed at her throat. "You look lovely today, Miss Shannon."

She flushed. "I hope you're not going to call me that all day. This is your day off."

"Yours, too."

"And we shouldn't spend it standing here," she objected lightly and turned to the Jeep door for escape from the magnetic pull of his charm. "We've got a long way to go."

"Yes, ma'am!"

Katie rolled her eyes as he swung around the Jeep to the passenger door and climbed in. "Tyler's place is farther away than the old homestead. It's on our property but at the very edge," she said, putting the key in the ignition. "We could ride there, but we'd spend the whole day in the saddle. And, seeing as you spent most of the week there, I thought you'd like a break."

"I appreciate that, but I already had a break yesterday. I went into Hancock with Mike."

"Mike Gardine?" She knew that Mike was the youngest ranch hand they had, and that he also lived in the bunkhouse. What she didn't know was that her newest hand and her youngest had become quick friends.

"He'd promised his mother to come into town for the afternoon, and I went with him."

Katie nodded. "His mother's a nice woman. I've met her. She has the best bakery in town."

"I know. I stopped in her store."

Katie caught his grin as she steered the Jeep out onto the range off the road and winced. First Lois Preston at the library, and now Betty Gardine at the bakery. Travis McCord was going to have every woman in Hancock wrapped around his finger if he kept smiling at them. "Got a free sample, did you?"

"Several."

Katie laughed. "And what did you do in town besides eat?"

"I went to the library."

She rolled her eyes. "Not again!"

"Miss Preston was glad to see me."

"I'll bet," Katie muttered under her breath, but Travis didn't hear.

"She gave me a library card and some books to read at night." Both of which had pleased him tremendously. Books had been a rare commodity back in Eagle River. To have a ready supply of them was a luxury he was going to enjoy getting used to.

"History again?"

"Yes. I have—"

"A lot to catch up on. I know." She shook her head. "The way you talk, I'm tempted to believe you've been asleep for the last hundred years."

"I have been, more or less."

She laughed and rolled her eyes as the Jeep bounced over the rolling terrain of the Double S. "Travis McCord, you are incredible!"

Seated beside her, Travis just grinned, and Katie had to grin back. It was impossible not to be affected by the infectious warmth of his smile.

"Okay, Sheriff McCord. You told me all about the people of the city of Eagle River. What about Tyler Fenton? He didn't live in the city. He just lived by it." She steered the Jeep around a cluster of rocks. "The only thing I really know about him was that he was kind of a hermit who claimed to have a lot of gold stashed away."

Travis shrugged. "That's about all there is. Tyler kept to himself. He never talked much to anyone. People used to say he was the first citizen of Eagle River, that he'd been living there long before anyone else arrived."

"During the gold rush?"

Travis shook his head. "Eagle River never experienced much of a gold rush. All the big mining camps were down in Bannock or over toward Helena. Eagle River had some deposits found and the first color brought a lot of people looking, but the mining here never brought more than a good living for the miners for a few years.''

"And Tyler?''

"If you could believe half his talk, he was rich.''

"No one ever saw him with any gold?''

"A little dust. A few nuggets. Nothing to make anyone believe he'd ever found anything big.'' Travis shook his head but suddenly frowned as old memories stirred. "Tyler was always out panning or digging somewhere. He never stopped looking for gold.'' Yet he'd always claimed to have buried plenty of it. More memories stirred.

"What about the other miners? They never saw Tyler with anything?''

Travis shoved the memories away. "No, but the big camps weren't that close to Eagle River. They were farther west, but as Eagle River was the closest town, that's where they came to celebrate and dance with the ladies.''

"And where they bumped heads with the ranchers.''

Travis grinned. "I don't think either the miners or the ranchers wanted to fight, but it seemed natural to them to resent each other. The townsfolk were probably the ones who started it all. They complained the miners were too rowdy when they came to town, and the ranchers just naturally backed the townsfolk up.''

"But without the miners coming to spend their gold in town, how would the townsfolk have made any money?''

Travis shrugged. "Doesn't make sense, does it? But the women were worried about the guns going off and the miners' intentions."

"Toward them?" Katie asked, wide-eyed.

"It just took one remark to the wrong woman by the wrong man who'd had a little too much to drink." Travis grimaced, remembering the woman. No one but a drunk would have made a pass at her. She'd had a face that could have broken glass. "Her husband got upset and started making threats, and everyone got riled up. Arguments started over simple things. If something was found missing from a store shelf, a miner got blamed. Then a steer turned up missing on the range." He shook his head. "That nearly started a war."

"Is that when Travis McCord came?"

Travis shifted uncomfortably in his seat. He wasn't used to talking about himself in the past tense, as if he was dead and gone—even though that was exactly what he should be. He looked at Katie. She trusted him. He wanted her to. But, while he believed he'd come forward in time to help her, how could he if he couldn't be honest with her? Yet what would she say if he told her the truth? Could he convince her without proof?

Drawn by his silence, Katie looked to Travis and found him staring at her. "Is something wrong?"

Travis shook his head sharply and gestured through the windshield ahead. "We're close."

She nodded and turned her gaze forward again. "Yes. I hope you won't be disappointed in Tyler's place. His property is on ours, but because it's so far away and we have no use for them, we never really kept the buildings up."

Travis didn't comment. Recognizing the slope of the land around him, he remained silent as his stomach knotted and his mouth abruptly went dry. They were driving toward Tyler's shack from the same direction he'd come with Molly and Billy all those years ago. His palms started to sweat. He was back where Molly's life had ended and his nightmare had begun.

"The barn's all but fallen down and the house's roof has caved in, but somehow they're both still standing," Katie went on, unaware of Travis's discomfort and hanging on to the steering wheel. The road that had once led to Tyler Fenton's place was no more. The way was paved with rocks and grass and unexpected dips instead. "Here we are," she said as the old buildings came into view.

When she brought the Jeep to a stop a short distance from the shack, Travis got out and stood with fists clenched, staring at the place where he had lost control of his life. The shack, run-down the day he and Molly had come with Billy, had decayed further. The walls were still steady, but one side of the roof had collapsed. The barn behind the shack was in worse shape. The whole building was leaning precariously to the left as if any minute a beam would snap and the walls would fall in. The corral where Tyler had kept his mules was gone. Only a few broken poles remained.

In stiff silence Travis slowly walked to the front door of the shack where he knelt to trail his fingers through the dirt. Time had erased the stains Molly's blood had left, but it hadn't dimmed the memory of seeing her stretched lifeless on the ground.

"That's where Molly was found," Katie said from behind him. "Billy told everyone later that she was shot as she tried to go through the door." Katie gestured to the right, though Travis couldn't see with his back to her as he continued to kneel. "Travis McCord was found over there by the corner of the shack."

Struggling to control the rage roaring through him, Travis stood and took a deep breath. Molly had died because of him. Billy had seen his own mother shot and killed because Sheriff Travis McCord hadn't done his job. Slowly he moved to where he remembered falling.

"One of the thieves was found a short distance from Travis. Billy said Travis shot the man when he came running. The second thief was found just inside the shack. He and Travis killed each other when they fired at the same time."

Without answering, Travis stared at the dirt where he had fallen, but he could feel no regret for his passing. He wasn't dead. Molly was. Silently he moved toward the barn.

Frowning, Katie watched him go. Something was wrong. Travis's back was stiff. His silence seemed almost angry. But why? Quickly she followed him. Yet when he went inside the sagging building, she hesitated. The barn could collapse at any moment. But suddenly she didn't want to leave him alone. Stepping inside, she found him once again kneeling.

"Tyler was found in here. Dead. The thieves had killed him before ransacking the shack. No one ever knew if Travis found Tyler before the shot. He may never have known what was happening or why."

"No." Travis stood.

"You think Travis found Tyler before the shot?"

"Yes."

Before she could say anything else, Travis abruptly turned on his heel and strode past her out of the barn. She hurried after him to catch his arm. "Travis, what is it?" But when his eyes met hers, she wasn't prepared for the hatred in his glare. Dark and bitter, it seemed to consume him. She released his arm and stumbled backward. "Travis?"

"I left Molly and Billy alone. I should never have done that! I should have known better! The shack's door was open. I should have checked inside, but I didn't. I left them alone and went out back to find Tyler." Travis swung to look at the barn. "His mules were in the corral. I figured he was in the barn getting hay for them when he didn't answer my call."

Katie watched Travis pace away, wanting to speak but not sure what to say, how to respond to the anger and anguish in his voice. He was talking as he had so many times before, as if he had been part of the past, but that couldn't be. Tyler Fenton had died over a hundred years ago. Yet Travis obviously believed what he was saying.

"When I got to the barn, I found him lying in the aisle. He was dead. Someone had hit him over the head, but his body was warm." Travis looked from the barn to the shack. "That's when I heard the shot."

Katie followed wordlessly as he strode to a place by the corner of the shack and gestured sharply.

"I didn't think like I should have. I just took off running instead. I charged outside and saw one of the thieves. We shot at each other. He missed. I didn't. He fell here."

Katie looked where Travis pointed and followed him as he stepped around to the front of the shack.

"That's when I made my second mistake. I should have stopped and come up to the front slow, but I heard Billy crying."

Katie touched his arm, alarm making her heart pound, but he didn't look at her.

"Molly was lying on the ground. Her dress was covered with blood. Billy was beside her, and the picnic basket she'd packed had spilled all over the ground." Travis took a deep breath.

She watched it shudder through him.

"I didn't see the second man. Not until it was too late. He was standing in the door, his gun up. We fired at the same time." Slowly Travis turned to face Katie. Her eyes were wide and filled with concern and disbelief, but that didn't stop him. He was going to tell her the truth. "I didn't know I'd killed him until you told me."

Chapter Five

Katie shook her head. What Travis was telling her wasn't possible. She shouldn't—couldn't—believe what she was hearing. But as she stared into his eyes, she didn't see the glitter of madness, only of determination. And the emotion she'd witnessed and heard had been real. His pain was real. "I don't understand."

The words were whispered, but they gave him the strength to continue. She hadn't said he was crazy. "I don't, either." He shrugged and pulled his hat off his head to run a hand through his hair. "You're the first person I've talked to since... since I killed Molly."

"No!" Katie jumped forward to grab him by the arms, anger overcoming her disbelief. "That's not true! What happened wasn't your fault!"

"It was. I should have been more cautious, not only for her sake but mine. I was a lawman. I shouldn't have run blindly. I could have taken cover, but when it came to her and Steve, I didn't have any sense. They were my friends—my family. If it hadn't been for them, I would have moved on once the trouble settled down in Eagle River, but because they made me feel like I belonged, I stayed."

Katie stared up at him, struggling not only with what he was saying but with the implication of his words. Ever since she'd met Travis, he'd talked as if he'd been part of the past, but what he said didn't make sense. He couldn't have known Steve and Molly. They had died over a hundred years earlier. Yet it was obvious he believed he'd been their friend. She stumbled for words. "It must have been hard to see Molly die."

His eyes darkened. "It was, but worse was waking up later at the cemetery. Everyone walked right by me as if I didn't exist. I thought they were all angry because I'd let her die, but then I saw my own tombstone."

Katie's fingers tightened on his arms. What he was saying couldn't be. He and Travis McCord of 1883 were two separate people. They had to be!

"After that I kind of flashed in and out for a hundred years." A wry grin pulled at his mouth, but sorrow lingered in his eyes. "I didn't understand why or where I was. I couldn't talk to anyone. Nobody could talk to me. Until you."

His eyes met hers, and her smile trembled. "You were surprised I could see you."

"About as much as you were to see me," he told her. "You almost jumped out of your boots."

"You came out of nowhere. What did you expect?"

"I didn't expect you."

The warmth of his gaze surrounded her, and her breath caught in her throat. Could he be telling the truth? She thought back to the way he'd talked about those who had lived in Eagle River. His stories had seemed so real, as if he'd seen the people, not only read or heard about them, and his wariness of modern equipment, his knowledge of the past and the way he sought always to learn about the present. Doubts of her own sanity made her light-headed. "You didn't recognize me right away? As being related to Molly?"

"No, I was too overwhelmed at being able to talk to and touch someone again. It wasn't until you took me up to the cemetery that I finally thought I understood what was happening."

She frowned. "You mean why you could see and talk to me?"

He nodded. "I thought I was being given a second chance."

"Second chance?"

"To somehow make up for what I'd let happen to Molly." His eyes searched hers. "You're why I'm here. I'm here for you."

The declaration almost buckled her knees, and she was nearly lost in the sincere strength of his gaze. But she had to break away. She needed to think. What he was saying couldn't be true, but she was starting to believe him and that was alarming. He couldn't be from the past. Yet she wanted to believe he was. She wanted to give in to his fantasy. Releasing her grip on his arms, she stepped back and tried to find reason, but her feelings were getting in the way. She was falling in love with Travis McCord, and that meant she wanted to find excuses for him.

Travis saw the doubt, recognized her uncertainty and understood it. He'd been doubting himself for years. Nevertheless, his jaw tightened. He needed Katie to accept who and what he was. "You don't believe me."

Katie's eyes flew to his, and with her mind whirling she searched for answers. Perhaps he'd been living and working with the past too long. He'd come to associate too closely with the first Travis McCord. "You believe it."

"You should, too."

Putting a hand to her head, she tried to overcome her faith and trust in him with logic. It didn't work. Too many things about him, his questions and comments, the way he approached everything. How many times had she accused him of acting as if he had lived in the past? And how many times had he tried to tell her that he had? But she hadn't listened. Hadn't wanted to. She licked suddenly dry lips and struggled to find the truth. "You shouldn't blame yourself for Molly's death."

"Molly shouldn't have died. She was young. She had a husband and a son."

The steel was back in his voice. And the pain. Katie pushed her confusion aside to rush to his defense. "What could you have done differently? Did you know someone was in the shack? Were there horses outside? Men loitering around? Any noise? Anything to make you suspect something was wrong?"

Travis frowned, staring back in time. "No."

"Then why shouldn't you have left Molly and Billy at the wagon?" Travis didn't say anything, and she stepped back to grip his arms once more. "You died coming to Molly and Billy's rescue." His eyes darkened and she quickly pushed on, "Listen to me. If you had checked inside first, what would have happened? You would still have died, the thieves would have gotten away and Molly—" Katie paused "—Molly wouldn't have been able to defend herself and Billy against two men, and I doubt they would have cared about what happened to her."

Travis stiffened. He'd always believed that he could have saved Molly. During the steady passage of time, going over and over what he'd done versus what he could and should have done, never once had he doubted that she would have lived and remained unharmed if he'd just gone into the shack first. But was that true? Would instinct and quick reflexes really have allowed him to shoot before being shot? Could he have killed the thieves before dying himself?

He was confident of his own abilities. He'd had to be to survive as a lawman. But he could have been killed instantly—just as Molly had been. He just didn't want to believe it because that meant Molly still would have been hurt. With him dead, she and Billy both could have been killed.

His fists clenched, and he nodded reluctantly. "Maybe you're right."

"I know I am." She stared up at him. He didn't sound convinced. "But you're still not sure."

Travis shook his head. "I keep thinking of Steve. He was a good friend."

"He didn't hold any grudges. Why should you?"

Travis smiled and lifted a hand to brush her hair away from her face. She was so fierce and concerned, so warm and appealing.

Abruptly Katie saw his eyes darken again and felt a sudden thrill when she realized she was the cause. His fingers dropped from her hair to trace the line of her jaw. His touch was gentle. She moved closer, and her hands drifted from his arms to his chest. The muscles beneath her palms were solid and strong under his shirt. His head started to lower toward hers, and she closed her eyes.

In height she didn't even reach his shoulders. In his arms she felt incredibly small and vulnerable. Standing as they were, her thighs brushed his, her breasts rubbed against his chest. She seemed to fit against him perfectly, and to kiss her seemed the only thing to do.

She trembled at the first feather-light touch of his mouth to hers. With his size, his strength, it wasn't what she expected. He surrounded her, but his caress was gentle. Soft. She wanted more. She leaned forward and found him waiting.

His mouth played over hers and his hands spread longingly over her back. Drawing her closer, he felt her arms slide up his chest to circle his neck, and lifted his head slowly to stare down into her face. Gold fire was dancing in the depths of her hazel eyes. He swallowed, knowing he should stop, but she pulled him back down to her and he was lost.

She murmured incoherently against his lips as her fingers caught in the hair curling around his collar, but somehow, even while the heat of their bodies seemed to meld them together, they drifted apart. Hands slid down arms, his savoring the soft feel of her skin until their fingers linked, and he found himself staring down at her in dazed wonder.

Never had he met a woman like her, but as Katie swayed toward him, Travis managed to hold her without bringing her back against him. Yet the temptation was strong. She was soft and tasted good, and it had been a long time—over one hundred years—since he'd felt the touch of a woman. But to touch her again meant losing control of the situation, and he couldn't do that. He had come to protect her, and he was going to do it. For Steve. For Molly and Billy. For himself. Katie Shannon was special. He wasn't going to let anyone change that.

To try to save them both from an awkward situation, he smiled and clipped her chin with a teasing finger. "Seems Travis McCord has gone from sheriff to thief, only he's not looking for gold."

Katie flushed under the all-encompassing blue of his gaze and backed reluctantly out of his grip. "I guess we both got a little too emotional."

He reached out to catch her chin. "You do believe me?"

The light of fear was in his eyes, and she hurried to reassure him, burying her own uncertainty. She didn't know how, couldn't comprehend why it had happened, but somehow it was true. He'd come from the past. For her. The idea left her breathless. "You said you'd never lie to me."

He smiled as relief shuddered through him and reached out to take her hand in his. "I won't."

She let him lead her back toward the Jeep, enjoying the warm strength of his palm against hers but wondering about him, about the past, about how the past could reach into the future. Doubts lingered in her head, but her heart kept saying it was true. He wasn't lying. Somehow, the impossible had happened. When he opened her door, she stopped to look back at the shack. "I guess we'll never know if Tyler Fenton really had any gold."

Travis frowned, and old memories stirred again. "The thieves believed he did." His frown deepened as he remembered visiting Tyler after the old man had been keeping company with a whiskey bottle. Tyler had been rambling about burying his gold where no one would think to find it. Travis shook his head. "I don't know why. Unless they'd seen something no one else had." Another memory stirred.

Katie sighed. "I don't think there was any gold. Otherwise Tyler would have done something with it besides hide it."

"Maybe." But suddenly Travis remembered stumbling on Tyler by the stream just beyond the shack. The old man had been surprised, unnaturally frightened at the unexpected intrusion. Travis frowned again. He'd thought Tyler was out panning for gold again and had been upset at having someone find the location of his newest "claim." Yet, oddly, Tyler hadn't had any of the usual mining hardware with him. He'd been dirty, but he hadn't been carrying any pans or picks. Not even a shovel.

Unaware of his thoughts, Katie watched him until his gaze suddenly locked again with hers. Disbelief was strong, but the truth was stronger. She was standing and talking to a man from the past. "The others will never believe you."

He shrugged. "They don't have to know. Only you do. I'm here to help you." His fingers reached up to brush her cheek. "I don't know how exactly, but we'll figure it out."

Swallowing against the desire to once again lose herself in his arms, she fumbled for the keys to the Jeep, but her hormones were jumping. It wasn't every day she had a man declare he existed only for her. The idea was a bit unsettling. Abruptly she yanked the keys free from her pocket and dangled them in front of him. "Want to drive?"

Travis stared at the silver ring and was sorely tempted to try, but he ended up shoving his hands into his pockets. "I don't know anything about cars."

She frowned and turned to stare at the Jeep, trying to see the same machine he did and realizing it had to be intimidating. "Cars are kind of like horses. You feed a horse to give it energy to go, and you use reins to guide it. With a car, you give it gas instead of food and use a steering wheel to make it go where you want."

"Gas?"

Katie's frown deepened. "It's liquid. You put it in the tank, and then when you step on the gas pedal, the gas makes the car go." She shrugged. "Actually, it's a little more complicated than that, but engines have what they call horsepower."

"Horsepower," Travis repeated and remembered Earl Carter's "V-8" engine.

Having gotten his attention, she lifted the keys once again. "Care to try?" And, when he continued to hesitate, teased, "What's wrong, Sheriff? Don't tell me you're afraid."

Pride had him reaching for the keys.

She grinned and ran around to the passenger's side. "Driving isn't that hard."

Not so sure, Travis climbed into the driver's seat with an equal amount of trepidation and joy and put the key in the ignition as he'd seen her do.

"The hardest part to remember is that this isn't an automatic. You have a clutch and have to use your right foot for the brake as well as the gas." She laughed at his puzzled expression—and at the way he sat behind the wheel. "But first I think you'd better adjust the seat so your knees aren't up around your neck!''

Laughing and shouting, it took three tries to get the Jeep started and rolling. Gears screeched in protest and the engine coughed as they went and the motor died again and again, but Travis didn't want to quit. Giving up just wasn't in his nature, and eventually, somehow, he got them away from the shack and out onto the meadows to spin around trees and rocks.

Katie squealed as his confidence grew and he steered the Jeep in elated circles in a vacant field and later gave chase to a rabbit going over a hill, and she screamed when he careened over a ledge on two wheels. But Travis was like a kid let loose with a brand-new toy, and the joy it gave him was contagious. She wasn't in danger of losing her life, only her heart.

"We're nearing the ranch, so watch out for people and animals as well as rocks," she warned hours later.

Travis grinned at her, pleased with himself and his progress, but when he had to shift to a lower gear, the Jeep shook and the engine whined as he gave it gas without direction.

"Let out the clutch!" she shouted, and screamed again as he wove through the yard toward the nearest building. "Don't hit the garage!"

Bringing the Jeep to an abrupt halt, he shut off the engine and held the keys out to her. "That wasn't too hard."

"Easy for you to say," she retorted, grabbing the keys and jumping out of the Jeep. "I didn't think we'd make it back in one piece! Maybe I'd better leave you in charge of the horses."

Smiling, he climbed out of his seat and put a hand over his stomach. "I'm starved. Did we miss lunch?"

Katie looked at her watch and nodded. "Afraid so. I can fix you something up at the house." But as they turned in unison, her footsteps suddenly faltered.

"You have company." Travis stopped beside her. "Know them?" he asked of the two men standing ahead waiting.

"Yes, it's Simon Griffith, my stepfather, and Ken Baxter." She shouldn't have been surprised to see them, but she was. With Travis's coming, somehow all of the other people she knew had been forgotten, but the moment hadn't yet come to think about what that meant. And the time wasn't right to wonder further about who he was. "Come on. I'll introduce you."

"There's my girl," Simon greeted her, holding out his arms for a big hug. "You out gallivanting again?"

"Yes. I took Travis to the old Fenton place."

"Don't tell me he likes that old stuff, too?" Simon asked and extended his hand to Travis. "Simon Griffith."

"Travis McCord." He accepted the handshake and nodded to the older man. Unlike Mark Harrison, her stepfather had warmth to him, and it was easy to respond to. "I understand you're Katie's stepfather."

"That I am."

"And I'm Ken Baxter," the second man put in, drawing everyone's attention to him. And, as Travis put his hand to his, added, "I'm Katie's fiancé."

If the man had hit him in the stomach with all his might, Travis wouldn't have been more stunned. Katie was going to marry this blond-haired, gray-eyed man with the firm handshake and a friendly smile!

"What's this?" Simon said with a laugh. "Is there something I don't know about?"

"There's something I don't know about!" Katie exploded. The announcement had shocked her at first, but anger was quick to take its place. Full-fledged, boiling fury. "Isn't it customary to ask the wife-to-be before making a proclamation?"

Looking down into her flushed face and flashing eyes, Ken Baxter tripped over a laugh. "I just thought—"

"No, you didn't think!" Katie lashed back. "That's your problem. You like to say things for their shock value and then sit back and watch to see where the chips land. Well, this time you've gone too far!" She whirled on Travis. "You'll excuse us, Travis, but I don't believe you're going to want to be part of a very loud argument."

As Travis watched her spin on her heel and march up the steps with the two men sputtering and running after her, he grinned. His relief at hearing her deny the announcement was strong enough to buckle his knees, but her temper was something he was glad to avoid. With a shake of his head, he turned toward the bunkhouse and its refrigerator. He hoped there was something good to eat inside because he was hungry, and it would be a couple of hours before supper.

"KATIE, I—" Ken began.

"What could you have been thinking?" she demanded, whirling to face him again as soon as they entered the house. "Making that kind of pronouncement without asking me first—and in front of a complete stranger!"

Ken shrugged. "Maybe I said it because I'd like it to be true."

"If that's a proposal, you're a little late. You're supposed to ask for my hand before you make an announcement!" she snapped and stomped off into the study.

Ken rapidly followed. "Look, I'm sorry if I embarrassed you, but you can't blame me for wanting to say something with the way your friend out there was hanging all over you."

"He wasn't even touching me!"

"Maybe not with his hands," Ken agreed. After being away for nearly a month, the homecoming he was having with Katie wasn't what he'd expected. "But he certainly had a gleam in his eye."

"A gleam . . ." She glared at him. "Your jealousy doesn't do you justice, Ken. Why don't you leave? You're not welcome here right now."

"But—" He turned to look at Simon, who was standing quietly to the side. "When I followed Simon out here, I thought we'd have supper. . . ."

"I suggest you go," Katie returned, crossing her arms in front of her as she faced him from behind her father's desk.

When Ken looked to him for help, Simon just shrugged and held up his hands. Ken turned back to Katie. "I'm leaving town again in a few days to go to a convention in Las Vegas. I thought you might like to come with me to get away for a while. If you feel like talking about it, call me when you're in a better mood." He whirled and headed for the door.

"In a . . ." She reached for a paperweight, but Simon put a hand up to stop her as Ken disappeared into the hall.

"It won't do any good. You'll miss him, and you're the one who's going to have to pick up whatever you break trying."

Katie's fingers curled around the multicolored globe. "I'm not in a bad mood."

"Really?"

Outside, a motor blasted to life and tires squealed as Ken Baxter backed up. From the bunkhouse window Travis grinned as he bit into an apple, but he didn't watch the slick sports car peel out of the yard. Instead his eyes went back to the house. One down.

"Don't you start!" Katie threatened Simon.

"I'm just an innocent bystander. I was as surprised by Ken's announcement as you," Simon told her. "But there was some truth to what he was saying."

Her eyes narrowed.

"Travis McCord was looking at you as if you were sort of special—not that that's bad," he hurriedly added. "Because it's true."

Pacified, she set down the paperweight and sank into the oversize chair behind the desk. She frowned and tried to picture the gleam that had allegedly been in Travis's eye. She hadn't seen it. But then, maybe the one he'd put in hers had blinded her to it. "Travis is a nice man, and he just happens to like history and Eagle River just as much as I do." Not to mention, he could kiss the socks right off her.

"Yes, Mark told me that your Travis said his last job had been as sheriff of Eagle River." Katie bolted up from where she had sagged in the chair. "He didn't come looking for me. We just ran into each other in town this week when he came in for some supplies."

"He didn't mention it."

"What's to mention?" Simon took a chair opposite the desk and hitched his pant legs up slightly to protect the creases as he sat. "He was a bit concerned about this new man. No one seems to know much about him."

Katie shrugged nonchalantly. "Maybe not, but he's a good hand. Even Mark has to recognize that."

"You like him?" Simon asked. "This Travis McCord?"

Katie rolled her eyes to the ceiling. "I just met him, Simon. I barely know the man." But what would she have done if he hadn't chosen to break the embrace? Scowling, she brought her eyes down to the desk and shuffled the papers on its top.

"That mean you'll give some thought to Ken's proposition? He'd like to show off, you know. He's very proud of what he does, traveling around the country—"

"Giving his expert advice."

Simon smiled at her sarcastic reply. "He likes you."

She shrugged. "Maybe, but I can't go." Didn't want to, because it meant leaving Travis. Her frown returned. How had she ever thought Ken attractive? Next to Travis, Ken didn't seem the same as he once had.

"Why not? It'd do you good."

"It's not a good time to leave the ranch. And I don't feel that way about Ken. He's nice, but being his consort doesn't appeal to me. Besides, think of the rumors it would start."

"Nothing wrong with rumors," Simon told her. "Adds a little spice to life."

She laughed. "Are you staying for dinner?"

"Maybe. But you're changing the subject. I think it'd still be good for you to go to Las Vegas with him—no strings or beds attached."

She flushed. "Simon! I said no!"

"Because of the ranch?"

She nodded.

"Problems?"

"No, I think they're solved." She took a deep breath. "I got myself a loan."

He blinked. "You what? But if something happens, you could lose the ranch!"

"And if you had given me a loan like you wanted and something happened, I'd lose the ranch and you'd lose your business." She shook her head. "A loan was the only way. Besides, my credit's good. The bank knows me and the ranch. They know its value."

He shook his head. "I understand this ranch means a lot to you, Katie, but I worry it's more than you can handle. Don't let pride stop you from doing what you've got to. You can still sell and move on."

"To where? This ranch is all I've ever known, and it's seen bad times before. And remember, Mom ran this ranch on her own for quite a while after Grandma and Grandpa died and before Dad arrived on the scene."

"Yes, but the ranch was in good shape then."

"It's in good shape now." She got up to move around the desk to him. "I've got a good foreman, even if he is arrogant, and I've got good people working for me. It might be tight now, but it'll get better." She bent to kiss his cheek. "Now stop worrying."

He sighed. "Tell me what we're having for dinner. I'm hungry."

Katie laughed as he stood and linked her arm with his. "Come on, let's go check out the freezer."

AT SUNSET the big silver car was still sitting in front of the house, but its presence didn't bother Travis. He hadn't gotten to say much to Katie's stepfather, but his first reaction to the man had been positive. Simon Griffith dressed in a fancy way, but he had a firm handshake and an honest enough face. And he was Katie's only family—outside the aunt Roxanne she'd mentioned on their first meeting. But as her mother's sister hadn't liked the ranch, it was doubtful she was anywhere around to be of any support to Katie.

Travis moved from the window to stare at the television set Mike Gardine was watching. Allegedly the picture came from the "satellite dish" out back, but danged if he could figure out how a big metal circle could turn air into pictures and put them into a small box. But it was entertaining. He walked to another chair opposite the television and sat down to open the book in his hand. He figured he could read and watch the TV at the same time, and maybe in the reading he could figure out what made the box work. Anything to take his mind off Katie. Especially after that kiss.

Travis frowned. He hadn't expected anything like that to happen. Though Katie Shannon had a face and figure to set a man's blood to racing, he hadn't given much thought to how she'd feel in his arms until she'd suddenly been there, and once done, it was difficult to forget. He opened the book in his lap. He was going to have to be more careful around her. He'd been alone a long time, and she was his only connection to a new world. He couldn't let those reasons be an excuse to complicate an already complicated situation.

But Katie was different. Strong and vulnerable at the same time, he felt drawn to her, and it had nothing to do with Steve's relationship to her. It was the woman Katie Shannon who appealed to him with her dancing eyes, soft lips and gentle disposition, but he couldn't let her appeal or his own past interfere with his intentions. If he was going to help her solve the problems she was having with the ranch, he had to remain detached emotionally and concentrate on her.

He was relieved that he'd told her the truth and that she seemed to accept it. She might have doubts, but it was important to him that he could be honest with her. He frowned. Yet she still hadn't been honest with him. She hadn't told him what was wrong with the ranch.

Frustration had him gritting his teeth. He couldn't help straighten things out at the ranch unless he knew what was wrong, and time could be running out. When he saw her again, he was going to have to get her to talk to him—before it was too late.

Chapter Six

"Look out!"

Katie jumped back as two men came racing out the kitchen door, and a rolling pin slammed into the wall behind them.

The two skidded to a halt, oblivious to her as they looked back into the room behind them. Abruptly, the kitchen door slammed.

Smothering a grin, Katie looked from Mike to Travis. Mike was nursing his hand, and Travis was brushing flour from his shirt. It didn't take much guessing on her part to know what had happened. They'd tried to raid the kitchen where Helen was baking up a storm in preparation for the upcoming fair. An annual event, Helen was always one of the main contributors when it came to food, and while she was baking, she didn't take too kindly to being interrupted, especially by those with greedy eyes and grasping fingers. Katie's grin widened. "If you two want to survive till Sunday, you'd better stay out of the kitchen."

"Aw, but Miss Shannon," Mike protested, his brown eyes wide and innocent as he turned to face her. "We're just trying to help. If we taste what's cooking, we can tell her how good it is and whether she should enter it in the contest.''

"The contest is just for pies, Mike. Not for cookies or cake." She looked at his hand. "How are the fingers?"

"She didn't break any."

"And how did you get involved in this particular fracas?" she asked, turning to Travis.

"Just trying to maintain the peace, ma'am."

"You're not doing a very good job of it, Sheriff."

He just grinned and waved to Mike. The younger man readjusted the Stetson he wore over his dark hair, then joined Gus, who was heading for one of the pickups on the other side of the yard. "He's a good kid."

She nodded. "He is, and he obviously likes you."

"The feeling's mutual."

Katie stood watching him with her arms wrapped around a paper bag filled with various goods. Over the past two weeks ranch duties had mostly kept them apart. During that time she'd seen too little of him, spoken to him not nearly enough and worried about him a lot. A man from the past come to the future. The doubts were strong against his story when he was out of sight. Even looking at him as he stood before her, it was hard to believe. He fit in so well. It was easy to believe he'd made it all up, but when she was feeling instead of thinking, she didn't have any doubts. "He tell you about the fair?"

"He mentioned it. So did Gus. Everyone gets the day off." Seeing Katie again after being away for a few days made it hard to concentrate on what she was saying. He'd been out mending fences with Mike and Gus and spending restless nights in a line shack. Constantly he'd worried that while he was gone she might need him and he wouldn't be there. Or, worse, Ken Baxter would be. He didn't like the jealousy, knew it shouldn't be, but it was impossible to deny. His need to help and protect her was getting more personal. While he was away he'd missed seeing her, talking to her, sharing time and the companionship that had quickly grown between them. He hooked his thumbs in his belt to keep himself from reaching out to touch her and wondered if she felt the same way.

"It's an annual thing. This time every year there's a big fair just outside of Hancock. They get a carnival to come in with some rides for the kids, and there are bake sales to raise money for any local charity and pie contests to see who cooks the best."

"Are you entering?"

Her nose wrinkled. "Pies aren't my specialty. Besides, I wouldn't stand a chance against Helen. She's won the contest five years running."

Travis glanced over his shoulder. "Makes me want to try the kitchen once more."

"Not if you value your life."

He laughed, but when his eyes met hers again, she looked to the ground.

"I want to apologize about the other day with Ken—"

"Forget it. It's none of my business."

She bit her lip. "Ken gets a little carried away sometimes."

"Seems like a nice enough man."

"Nice enough to be my husband, you mean?"

It was Travis's turn to look down. "If that's what you want."

"It's not."

The strength of her statement brought his gaze back up.

She smiled at the relief in his eyes but said nothing about it. The warmth his reaction caused was enough. "He gets a little impressed with himself once in a while."

"If a man likes a woman, he likes to impress her."

She made a face. "You sound like Simon."

"Simon wants you to marry Ken?"

"Simon introduced me to Ken, but Simon only wants me to do what makes me happy."

Travis said nothing but continued to stare at her. It was hard to remember his good intentions when she looked as good to eat as anything he'd seen in the kitchen. The sunlight was dancing across her face and glinting off the blond hair that she'd pulled back into a ponytail, and her eyes were shy and watchful. He swallowed as the urge to step forward to touch her grew stronger.

"I'd best get this in to Helen," she said, feeling the heat rise in her cheeks under his steady scrutiny. Things between them were happening too fast. She'd promised herself to be calm and in control when she met him again, but her body wasn't honoring her wishes. She kept remembering how it had felt to have his arms around her.

Automatically he put a hand to his hat and stepped aside as she passed.

"If I don't see you before, I'll see you at the fair." The words were said over her shoulder.

"I'll look forward to it," he told her. "You can tell me what's best to buy at the sale."

She stopped to look back at him, suddenly reluctant to go. "You're getting along all right at the bunkhouse? I mean, there's nothing you need?"

"I'm fine." He recognized her uncertainty, but she was fighting any doubts. That meant she still believed him. She just wasn't certain what to do about it. "Things haven't changed that much. Besides, Mike and Gus keep me straight."

"And Mark?"

"We get along."

It was a reserved answer, but she'd expected no less. Her foreman wasn't very popular. "Good."

She started to turn, but he stopped her. "And the house?" They needed to talk, but it would have to be more than as polite strangers. He had to keep her trust, her interest, if he was going to get her to rely on him. He couldn't just be an oddity, someone out of time.

Her eyes drifted past him to the building she had once shared with her family. "Big and lonely sometimes, but it's getting better."

"I'm glad."

She nodded and licked her lips in a self-conscious gesture.

He followed the motion with hungry eyes and wondered if she thought about the kiss half as much as he did.

When his gaze settled on her mouth, she felt suddenly breathless. "I've got to go."

"Me, too." Travis turned and almost ran into Mark Harrison.

The foreman's gaze dropped to take in Travis's flour-splattered shirt. "Looking for something to do, McCord?"

"No, sir. I'm heading for the barn."

"Then get to it. You're not being paid to stand around." Thus issuing a dismissal, Harrison moved past Travis to tip his hat to Katie. "Morning, Miss Shannon. Can I help you with that bag?"

Travis resisted the urge to turn around to say or do something he might regret. Instead he satisfied himself with a quick clenching of his fists before he walked away, but the urge was there. He wanted to put his fist in the foreman's face, and it took him the rest of the day to work that desire out of his system.

"YOU READY FOR SOME PIE?" Mike asked, stopping to jab Travis in the ribs.

Travis's gaze dropped from the machine called a Ferris wheel that was going around and around in the summer sun carrying people who were squealing and laughing in swinging metal seats. It was Sunday, and since leaving church and reaching the fairgrounds, he'd sampled more types of food than he could remember—some of which he'd never heard of. Hot dogs, hamburgers, cotton candy, tacos, crepes, bratwurst, ice cream on a stick. But before he could answer Mike, his attention was caught by two young women. They were dressed in halter tops and shorts against the summer heat, their legs long and slim. He tipped his head to one side as he watched them pass. "Beats the hell out of gingham."

"What?" Mike asked, staring after the pair himself.

But Travis didn't try to explain. He just smiled and put a finger to his hat when the women looked back over their shoulders at him. It was the only polite thing to do.

"That new ranch hand of yours is going to have every woman in Hancock after one of those smiles of his," Helen Henry told Katie as she followed the younger woman's gaze to the tall figure standing beside Mike Gardine a short distance away.

"That one could knock a girl's socks off, all right," Mary Clarke agreed.

Katie felt uncomfortable heat rise in her cheeks as she stood between the two women behind the booth, where they were guarding and selling local bake goods to anyone who passed.

"I know," Katie finally agreed, her gaze leaving the masculine figure in question to go to the objects of his interest. A pang of jealousy hit her instantly as she saw the long legs and the tall, slender bodies, and she cursed fate for damning her to a height of five foot two and a half. She scowled. If he'd come forward in time for her, he shouldn't be ogling other women. Her gaze returned to him in censure, but resentment quickly vanished when she suddenly found herself pinned by his blue gaze. A dazzling smile was sent her way, and Katie felt her heart skip and her blood race. It was hard to stay mad at a man who could turn her knees to water with a single look.

"And here he comes," Helen said.

"I'm ready," Mary declared and earned a laughing scowl from Helen.

"Mary, you *are* married," Helen reminded her.

"Yeah, but I ain't dead." She turned all her attention to the two men approaching. "Howdy, cowboys. What can we convince you to try today?"

Both men tipped their hats, but Mike was the first to let his eyes drop to the rows of cookies, cakes, pies and other baked goods scattered across the booth shelf. "It's mighty hard to decide, Mrs. Clarke, with so much to choose from."

"What about you, Travis?" Helen asked, not missing the way his eyes lingered on Katie. She smiled at his interest. Katie could do worse.

"Well, ma'am, I have it on good authority that your pie is the best around," Travis told her, pulling his eyes from Katie.

Helen flushed happily, and her thoughts scattered abruptly at his flattery. "And what kind would you like? Apple? Peach? Cherry?"

Travis put a hand over his stomach in anticipation. "Why don't you give me your favorite?"

The words were followed by one of his smiles and, watching, Katie felt jealousy's sting again as Helen quickly raced to do his bidding. "Travis McCord, you could charm a flea right off a dog, as my grandma used to say."

He grinned and moved to stand opposite her at the booth. She was wearing jeans and a white ruffled blouse with a scooped neck that left the long column of her throat bare. Her hair was pulled back from the sides of her face with bright barrettes, and as she looked up at him, her hazel eyes danced with the golden flecks he remembered so well. "My mother always said smiles and compliments are free, and we should give them as often as we can."

"Sounds like quite a lady."

"She was." He glanced around the booth as Helen finished cutting his piece of pie and Mike pointed out his choice to Mary. "You have to work all day?"

"Just for a few hours."

"Maybe you can show me around later?"

Katie never got a chance to answer. Two young women sidled up to boldly confront Travis and Mike. Tall and long limbed with tanned skin and playful eyes, the first looked from Mike to Travis. "Mike, how's it going? Who's your friend?"

"Yeah, who's your friend?" the second woman asked. She was as tall as the first and as slim, and her hand was quick to take possession of Travis's arm. Katie hated her instantly.

"Annie," Mike stammered, "this is Travis. Travis, this is Annie and Suzanne."

Fuming silently, Katie found herself forgotten as the two women led the men off once the food had been paid for. And, her jealousy didn't die as the afternoon passed. Again and again she caught glimpses of Travis and Mike, usually in the company of women who were hanging on to their every word, if not some part of their anatomy.

When her turn in the booth was finally over, she was anxious to be gone, and left its confines wondering if she could convince Simon to take her home. He'd driven her to the fair, and with her feelings for Travis tying her up in knots, the need to flee was strong. Trapped in or out of time, he was more than she was prepared to handle.

Strolling through the grounds, she saw Simon across the way surrounded by a group of men from town. Ken Baxter was among them, and from the animation accompanying the conversation it was easy to see all were thoroughly engrossed in whatever topic they were discussing. She sighed and turned away. Escape was not to be. It looked as if she was in for a long night.

"I was wondering when I'd find you."

Katie turned to find Travis and watched him gesture to the empty shelves in some of the booths.

"Most of the food's gone."

"By the time the night's over, I'm sure all of it will be." She tried to resent his presence, remembering his flirtations of the afternoon, but it was hard to hang on to her jealousy when he was standing beside her instead of somebody else.

"I suppose I had more to eat than you."

His eyes seemed to devour her, and her gaze dropped even as her pulse jumped. "I suppose so." She looked up again to find him watching her. "Find anything you didn't like?"

"Nope." He grinned. "But running's hard work."

"Mike got you to join the footraces?"

"We won, too."

She laughed. "And where's Mike now?"

"Trying to find a young lady to give his prize to."

She stared at his empty hands. "You already found someone to give your prize to?" Her disappointment hurt.

He grinned. "I gave mine to Mike. Two prizes are a lot more impressive than one."

Laughter bubbled from her throat, and she gazed up at him, completely oblivious to the hawker a few feet away calling for them to come to try his game. She saw and heard only Travis, who was suddenly reaching out to pull her close. The heat of his hands burned her arms, and when he smiled she knew he was going to kiss her. She held her breath.

"Katie."

Jumping away with a guilty start, she turned to find Ken Baxter standing beside her. "Ken, I thought you were with Simon."

"I was just waiting to find you," he told her, his glare dark as it lingered on Travis. "I promised I'd win you a prize at the pitching booth, remember?"

"Oh, I . . ." She looked from Travis to Ken and found them staring at each other instead of at her. Another disadvantage of being short. "I guess you did."

Ken reached out to take her arm, pulling her away from Travis and toward the booth and the smiling hawker before she could protest. But Travis wasn't about to be left behind.

"Maybe we can win two prizes," Travis said and put his money on the counter.

The men's gazes again went over Katie's head. For them she'd ceased to exist. They saw only each other. But the hawker winked at her. He recognized a challenge when he saw it, and it was his job to take advantage of it. He grinned and handed each man three balls. "Let's see who gets the first prize for the little lady."

"WE HAVE A REGULAR competition going here, I see," Simon said, coming to a stop beside Katie and throwing her an amused look some time later. Her arms were filled with dolls and stuffed animals. She wore gaudy jewelry around her neck and wrist, and a hat with a feather adorned her head.

Katie flushed as she met his grin and caught laughing looks from others around her. "This is embarrassing," she told him in what was meant to be a hoarse whisper, but with all the noise from the games and crowd around her, her words were more of a shout. "I can't get these two to stop!"

The first competition had led to a second and a third. Travis and Ken had tossed balls, rings and used squirt and air guns to shoot at targets, yet despite the numerous prizes they'd won, neither was inclined to quit.

Simon put a comforting arm around her shoulders. "Enjoy it, girl. This is what life's all about."

Katie burst out laughing and stood with him to watch Travis and Ken approach yet another hawker. The two were entirely different in appearance and manner. One was dark, the other light. One calm but determined, the other flamboyantly arrogant in trying to win. Together they stopped to talk to a loud and grinning game promoter who stood in front of a tower with a huge bell hung at the top. The object of the game was to hit the pad at the bottom of the tower with a hammer hard enough to make the attached gong fly up to ring the bell.

"Who's winning?"

"They're tied." It was hard to remember exactly who'd won what, but she knew the jewelry was from Travis and the hat from Ken. Ken had also gotten her a multicolored stuffed turtle and a furry lion. Travis had added a unicorn and a long-eared purple rabbit.

"It can't last much longer," Simon assured her as Ken stepped up with the hammer in hand.

"Why not?"

"They're running out of games. And Ken's got to go. He's got a plane to catch in the morning."

Katie watched Ken test the weight of the hammer and give it a trial swing. Dressed in a white silk shirt with appropriate Western trim, he looked somehow out of place in the festive grounds. Around him everyone else wore faded jeans and T-shirts, but he was in silk and polyester. Yet while slender in build and slightly shorter than Travis, Ken kept himself in shape with regular visits to city health clubs, so when he brought the hammer down, the gong flew skyward.

She held her breath as it approached the bell. But its momentum was quickly lost, and the gong stopped just short of the bell and fell back to earth with a thud. Her eyes went quickly to Travis, who gave a disbelieving shake of his head before stepping forward to take the hammer.

Unlike Ken, he blended in with his surroundings. His shirt was blue cotton, his jeans were worn around the edges and his boots were scuffed, and there was plenty of power in his shoulders as he hefted the hammer to test its weight.

The crowd gathered around the tower grew quiet as Travis readied himself. Abruptly his shoulders flexed, the hammer came down and a loud thunk sounded. Gasps came from the people watching as the gong hurried upward. Katie bit her lip and squeezed her prizes as the gong's ascent began to slow. Defeat seemed certain, but the blow had been just enough. The gong hit the bell, a metal clang rang out and a cheer went up.

A grinning Travis gave the hammer back to the hawker and turned to shake hands with a slightly demoralized Ken before accepting a white bear that seemed nearly as big as he was.

At Ken's approach, Simon held out a hand. "Good try, Ken, but you'd best keep an eye on the clock if you're going to make that plane."

Ken nodded, sobered by defeat, and fixed Katie with an unfathomable stare. "I'll be gone for a while. I'll call when I'm back in town."

She smiled and accepted his kiss on her cheek in silence. She wanted to say something, but it was difficult to find any words, especially when her arms were full of dolls and toys and when the man she really wanted to kiss her was standing nearby.

Ken looked from her to Travis and gave a curt nod before moving away. Once he was gone, Simon stepped forward to take the white bear with the bright pink bow around its neck from Travis's arms. "You'd better give me that. I don't have a lady escort for the night, and it looks like Katie's already got her hands full."

Travis grinned and handed over the bear.

"You dance, cowboy?" Simon asked, throwing Katie a wink.

"I've been known to," Travis answered.

"Then you'd best get this young lady up to the tent yonder. They'll be calling square dances most of the night."

Katie watched Simon walk off with a wave, an elegant man with an oversize teddy bear trapped in his arms, but when her eyes came back to Travis, it was to find him studying her.

"I like the hat," he told her. "Especially the feather."

She laughed. "You must have lost a week's wages for this."

Travis just grinned. "It was worth it."

A soft flush filled her face as he continued to stare, but a loud whisper had her turning away from him. Nearby a little boy and girl stood gazing with wonder at the multitude of prizes caught in her arms. With a laugh, she fell to her knees.

Travis was quick to join her and plucked two toys from her arms.

A red dog went to the little boy, the purple rabbit to the girl. But, the first two children were quickly followed by others, and in no time everything was gone except the jewelry around Katie's neck. Yet she didn't mind.

Laughing, she watched Travis stand, and accepted his hand as he helped her to her feet. His fingers immediately linked with hers, and he turned to lead her in the opposite direction from the tent filled with people and music. She didn't object. Instead, she followed him willingly into the crowd, ready to go wherever he wanted to take her.

Chapter Seven

"You can't come to the fair without going on the Ferris wheel!"

Travis didn't have a chance to agree or disagree with Katie. Before he could decide if he wanted to go or not, she had the tickets in her hand and was leading him up the ramp and into a seat.

Thus far they'd spent the evening wandering over the fairgrounds eating cotton candy, going through the House of Mirrors and strolling among the crowd. He'd stopped often to stare in rapt wonder at the multicolored blinking lights of the various rides and to listen in amazement to the squealing people on them, but the Ferris wheel was the first ride Katie had tried to convince him to go on.

The metal bar was locked across their laps, and Travis gasped as the motor started and the wheel turned. Grabbing the bar as his stomach was left on the ground, he nearly closed his eyes when the wheel jerked to a halt and their car began swinging madly as someone got off below them and another couple got on.

Swallowing hard against the fear, he leaned forward to risk a look down but quickly sat back again.

Heights had never been a problem for him. He'd been over the mountains and across precarious ledges any number of times, but at least then he'd had a rock to hang on to that was connected to a solid wall.

Unaware of his dilemma, Katie gazed out at the fairgrounds spread below them. "Isn't it beautiful?"

His stare of disbelief went unnoticed as he turned to look at her, but nonetheless he followed her gaze to the brilliant spectacle below. The booths and the people had shrunk in size, but the colored lights made a spectacular display. Yet before he could comment, the wheel started to move again, and he was suddenly spinning through the sky.

As he hung on to his hat and the bar, the lights blurred, his stomach flipped and the cool evening air fanned his face. Fear was quickly replaced by exhilaration at the sensation of flying, and he laughed with Katie as they swooped from the ground to the sky repeatedly. Yet without warning their speed slowed, and the wheel came to a stop, leaving them stranded at the very top.

The car swung back and forth, and Katie laughed. "This is my favorite ride. I used to make my father take me on it again and again when I was a little girl." But she wasn't with her father anymore, and the man beside her didn't make her feel little. With him, she felt all grown up.

"I can see why," Travis murmured, but the ride was far from his mind as he gazed at her. The distant shine of the lights below seemed to float up and surround her with a halo, to caress her windblown hair and flushed cheeks. He knew he shouldn't do it, but he reached out to tuck a loose blond strand behind her ear.

Abruptly Katie became conscious of the warm length of his leg resting against hers, of the power of his shoulders and the smallness of the car they were in. High above the earth, it was as if they were alone in the world. Unconsciously she leaned toward him.

Warning bells went off. Kissing her wasn't what he should be doing. He was supposed to be asking her about the ranch. He bent his head, and his lips closed over hers.

The sweet smell and taste of her filled his senses as his hand skipped over her ribs to pull her more closely to him on the seat. He could feel the mad pound of her heart beneath his palm. It matched the wild pace of his own. He tried to pull her closer still but the unexpected jerk of the wheel plunged the car back toward the earth, and they separated with a cry as the wheel made one last dizzying circle before their car swung to a halt at the ramp.

The bar was lifted, and they ran away from the wheel but not from each other. Instead, laughing, they let the crowd carry them to the Chamber of Horrors.

Katie clung to Travis's arm as they went up the ramp, and she continued to watch him look around. Throughout the evening as they'd wandered together she'd made a conscious effort to try to see the carnival as he, a man out of time, might, but it hadn't been easy. When he was holding her hand she found it hard to remember anything about where he'd come from. Where he'd been before didn't matter. It was where he was that counted. With her.

It was dark inside the horror chamber, and Katie slowed as she led the way around the first turn. Travis followed, unprepared and unexpecting the skeleton that suddenly leapt out of the blackness. He yelled and

knocked her aside as his hand slapped his bare thigh
instead of the Colt he was after.

Bouncing off a wall, Katie swung to protest but
stopped when she found him staring in horror at the
illuminated man of bones. She was tempted to laugh,
but fear was no laughing matter. Smothering her
mirth, she went back to him. "It's not real, Travis.
The bones are made of plastic."

"Plastic?"

She reached out to flick one of the rattling "bones"
with her finger. "This is the Chamber of Horrors. It's
full of things that are supposed to scare people." And,
as if in confirmation, up ahead of them somewhere in
the dark, someone screamed. "See? This is supposed
to be fun."

"Fun!" he objected in disbelief.

She rolled her eyes and grabbed his arm. "Come on,
Sheriff. Let's see what's waiting to ambush us around
the next bend."

Uncertain but curious, Travis followed her again
and quickly found himself confronted by one ghoul
after another. Unsuccessfully trying to brace himself
for the unexpected, time after time he jumped as various images leapt out of nowhere. Considering he'd
never been in a horror chamber before, he supposed
that was normal. At least he liked to think it was.

More intent on watching Travis than where she was
going, Katie stumbled on through the blackness, feeling her way forward while looking back to see his next
reaction, until a turn in the maze suddenly had a
gnarled face shooting out at her. Caught by surprise
and squealing in alarm, she threw herself into Travis's
arms.

Grinning, he caught her, relieved to see her composure shattered at last, but when he looked down to find her face close to his, any teasing remark was lost as his eyes met hers.

Clinging to him, she felt the heat of his body blending with hers, and she forgot where they were. The startled cries, the mechanical noises, the boxed laughter were all lost to her. She was aware only of him and the warm blanket of darkness holding them together. "Travis."

Her whisper was the only thing he heard. Mindless to the sounds and to the others sharing the blackness with them, she was all he felt and saw, and before he realized what he was doing, he was bending to taste her lips.

She sighed as his mouth captured hers, and curved herself against the hard length of his body. In his arms was where she wanted to be, so she didn't object when he crushed her to him.

The year, the date, the time. He couldn't remember any of them. Why or how they had come together wasn't important. The only thing that mattered was that he was a man and she a woman, and she was melting in his arms.

Pinned against him, she felt as if she was being absorbed. His skin was warm, his touch hot. Her fingers tangled in his hair.

He cupped her head in his palm before tracing the line of her throat to the base of her neck. Her skin was softer than he could have imagined. He took his mouth from hers to taste it.

Gasping as his lips sought to explore new ground, she clung to the width of his shoulders. This was what she needed. Him wanting her. She pulled his head back so their mouths could meld once more, and her hands moved slowly up his chest, savoring the strength hidden beneath cloth and flesh.

His hands were moving, too, following the curve of a hip, exploring the small of her back, and abruptly finding the fullness of a breast. He swallowed her startled moan and felt desire surge through his veins. She was his. He'd come for her. His hands pressed her to him, and the softness of her breasts yielded against the width of his chest. He shuddered.

"Travis." His name was a whisper, a plea, but before she could ask for what he wanted to give, an unexpected blow sent her staggering.

Travis tightened his arms around Katie, keeping them both standing as they turned to face the two children who had come careening through the blackness and run into their legs.

Unaffected by the unexpected collision, the little girl met Travis's and Katie's startled stares with a puzzled frown. "Are you lost?" she finally asked.

"It's easy to get lost," the boy with her sympathized before Katie or Travis could respond. "But we can lead you out."

Struggling for words, Katie looked from the children to Travis. His eyes were still smoldering with the heat of passion and his grip on her was still strong, but they were in a public place. "We're not—"

"We know the way," the girl interrupted. "Come on."

"Yeah," the little boy agreed, and before either Katie or Travis could protest, they were being hurried out of the darkness and back into the bright lights of the fair.

NEVER HAVING THOUGHT of the Chamber of Horrors as a particularly romantic place, Katie was ready to revise her thinking as she hummed to herself the next morning while sitting beside Mark in the pickup truck. They were going to the west range to check on the stock that had been gathered a few days before in preparation for the roundup, but her mind really wasn't on where they were going. She was remembering where she had been.

Smothering a sigh, she thought again of the heat of Travis's embrace. His hands, his lips, his strength. If they hadn't been interrupted . . . She smiled to herself as the truck bounced over the uneven ground. It was just a shame the night couldn't have lasted longer.

"We're almost there," Mark commented.

Katie nodded silently. The line shack where they'd unload the mustangs from the trailer they were pulling so they could go ahead on horseback wasn't much farther. She sighed again and wondered where Travis was.

After leaving the chamber they'd gone to the tent and the dancing, but they hadn't been able to stay together there long. As late as it had been, everyone had been preparing to go home, and she'd had to leave the same way she'd arrived. With Simon. Travis had been left to return with Mike and the other men.

She remembered the ride back to the ranch and sitting beside Simon in his silver car while hugging the big white bear. She'd put it and the gaudy jewelry Travis had won for her carefully away before going to bed.

As they crested a hill, the line shack came in view. "We're here," Mark announced.

Katie straightened in her seat and frowned when she saw another truck parked outside the building. "Someone else is out here?"

"Checking fences," Mark agreed. "Won't do us any good to round up the cattle if all the fences aren't in good shape."

The pickup came to a stop beside the other truck, and Katie quickly hopped out and made her way to the back of the trailer. Mark joined her almost immediately, but when the gate was down and she was about to step inside, a deep voice stopped her.

"Why don't you let me get your horse out for you?"

Katie's heart leapt into her throat as she turned to face the man who'd appeared behind her. "Travis."

The word was almost a sigh, and he smiled in response. The last person he'd expected to see out on the range was Katie, but her arrival was a surprise he was prepared to deal with. He tipped his hat and stepped past her into the trailer. "We just finished our sweep of the fences to the south," he said as he backed her horse outside at the same time Mark did his. "We were about to head on up the north side of the range."

"We'll ride along," Mark said with a nod. "We want to have a look at the herd."

"Funny thing about that," Travis commented as he stopped the horse beside Katie. "There's an awful lot of loose cattle wandering hereabout. Considering the preliminary drive we made last week to flush out any stock, it doesn't seem right that there should be many strays. The only reason we stopped back at the shack was to call in and ask if you wanted us to keep on the fence or work the cattle."

Mark frowned as he tightened his cinch. "Gus and Mike with you?"

Travis nodded toward the shack. "Here they come now."

Mark moved off to greet the two men, and Katie watched Travis turn his attention to her horse and its cinch. Yet it was difficult to concentrate on business when he was so close and the memory of being in his arms was fresh. She cleared her throat. "There were a lot of cattle?"

"More than there should be if they were just strays that didn't get caught in the first run." He dropped the stirrup and gave her a winning grin. "No cause to worry."

But the way her heart thumped against her ribs when she was caught by his smile was worry enough. It was a struggle to keep her knees locked and a grip on the saddle horn as he gave her a lift up. His hand stopped to linger on her thigh once she was seated, and the heat of his touch burned its way through her jeans to her skin. "Thank you," she told him, too conscious of the other three men swinging into saddles nearby.

Travis tipped his hat again. He liked the way her eyes darkened, her cheeks flushed and her voice grew breathless when she was near him. It assured him that he wasn't the only one who was affected by their visit to the chamber that was supposed to hold nothing but horrors. "My pleasure, ma'am."

As one, all five riders swung their horses away from the shack and out toward the range and the waiting herd. The land between them and the cattle was rolling, but Katie frowned as she saw cattle scattered across the fields. "Could something have spooked the herd?" she asked Gus, who was riding to her right.

"I suppose," Gus conceded. "But I don't know what it could have been."

Katie didn't either, but as she watched the number of stock scattered about grow, a gnawing fear came to claw at her stomach. Something wasn't right. Once gathered, the herd would have drifted, but nothing short of a stampede would have seen the steers end up so far apart.

They came to a rise in the land. Together they crested the hill, prepared to see the herd stretched out below them, but the cattle weren't there. Or, rather, only one was.

"No," Katie murmured in disbelief as she stared at the steer. Stretched out on the ground, it lay perfectly still in the grass, but that wasn't the worst of it. A few feet from the dead animal stood the fence. A gaping hole had been cut into it, and a pole had been knocked out of its length. "No!"

Stunned, the men riding with her didn't move, didn't speak until she slammed her heels into her horse and went racing down the hill. They followed in unison, sliding to a halt and swinging from their saddles as she fell to her knees beside the lifeless steer.

Katie reached out a trembling hand toward the fallen animal. Blood stained its neck from where a bullet had been put through its skull. "Who did this? Who?"

Mike was the only one who seemed able to find his voice, as he stood with the others staring down at the heavy tire tracks that marred the earth where the fence had been cut. "Rustlers. It was rustlers who took our cattle."

Stunned, Katie was oblivious to the orders Mark barked out. She didn't see the men separate and ride off, didn't hear their words. She only felt a sense of doom.

Moments later Travis returned to where she still knelt by the steer. He and Mike had made a quick sweep of the area, following the truck's trail out and away from the Double S range to the road beyond, but as he slipped from the saddle to stare down at her, he was having a hard time grasping what was happening.

Rustlers he knew and understood. He'd chased and dealt with them before, but that was when they'd been on horseback and he'd been able to follow them. Pursuing these rustlers was an impossibility. They may have left a trail off the range, but how could anyone track a truck once it reached a cement highway?

"How many?" Katie finally asked when the men had regathered. Her face was white and her voice flat.

"Hard to say," Mark said, looking around him. "Usually one truck will hold about thirty head. They must have scattered the rest."

Gus spat into the dirt. "They're probably in another state by now."

"There must be a way to track them!" Travis snapped, frustration feeding anger as he watched a stricken Katie.

"Yeah, Sheriff McCord? How?"

Her foreman's sarcastic retort brought Katie to her feet. "Stop it! Stop it right now!"

Gus quickly stepped into the breach and between the two men. Travis had taken a lot of ribbing about his last job since his arrival, but it wasn't the time or place to discuss his former employment. "There ain't no way to track them, Travis," Gus answered while Travis and Harrison glared at each other. "These thieves got stealing down to a fine art. They get forged papers to get the cattle through weigh stations or past any law officers that might stop them."

Katie rose and walked to the fence to stand. Thirty head. She stared out at the tire marks that sat deep in the dirt. "When did it happen?"

"From the tracks," Gus said, coming to stand beside her, "I'd say Saturday late. Probably just before sunset so they could see what they were doing."

"No one would question a truckload of cattle on a Saturday around here," Harrison acknowledged, and frowned at Travis. "We'd better call this in to the real sheriff."

"No!" Katie denied before anyone else could speak or Travis could react. All the men turned to look at her in surprise. She didn't return their amazed stares but remained with her back to them at the fence. "As Gus said, they're in another state by now. What good will reporting it do?" And when no one spoke, she quickly continued, "Besides, this is probably an isolated incident. It happened once. It won't happen again."

Travis's gaze was sharp on her. Something was wrong besides the rustlers. She wouldn't look any of them in the eye.

"But—"

"I said no, Mark." She turned to face him and saw his nostrils flare in defiance.

"What about the other ranchers? They should know about this."

"I'll call Ed tonight," Katie told him. "He's got the only other spread close to the highway like we are." But the rustlers had picked on the Double S. They'd gone after her cattle instead of someone else's. Her eyes returned to the dead steer.

"She's right," Gus said, backing her up. "Won't do any good to report it. The thieves won't get caught, and I've never heard of them striking the same ranch twice. Too risky."

"Has this happened before?" Travis asked, turning to the older hand as Katie's eyes lifted to him. It was tearing him apart, not being able to go and hold her, but it was time for rational thinking, not emotion.

"Once quite a few years back before Katie's father died but never since." Gus nodded to Katie and frowned as he remembered. "That was over on the north range, though, and Ed Peck's place up the road got hit at the same time."

"Yes," Katie agreed. "The sheriff thought that it was one group who came with two separate trucks."

"They get as many head then?"

Gus grunted. "More."

"But where do they take them? Sell them?" Travis prodded. "Surely some of them have been caught?"

"Not often," Gus responded. "But as to where they sell them, I suppose they take them to some slaughterhouse or to another rancher who's not so picky about where his new stock comes from."

Katie watched Travis grapple with the facts. He was trying to help, trying to understand, but he was out of his depth as well as out of his time when it came to modern-day rustlers. In 1994 more rustlers stole and got away with it than were hauled into court. She turned to her oldest hand and gestured to the fallen steer. "Gus, do you think you can take care of this for me?"

"Yes, ma'am, and we'll fix the fence."

Katie nodded but kept her head down. She didn't want to see any of their faces, to answer any questions, to acknowledge any of her own fears by telling them they were right. The county sheriff should be notified, but she couldn't let that happen. Forcing herself to remain calm, she turned back to her horse and away from the men, but she could feel Travis's eyes on her as she went. She longed to look at him, but if she did, she'd be tempted to walk into his arms and that was something she couldn't do. He was her ranch hand. She was his boss. And he was as helpless as she to bring back her stolen stock. "Mark, let's go. There's nothing more we can do here."

The three hands stood silent as Katie and Mark remounted and rode away, but Gus spoke before they were out of sight. "We'd best get going, too, if we're going to take care of this and get back to the ranch by sunset."

THE TASTE OF DEFEAT was bitter for Travis as the pickup truck bounced into the ranch yard hours later and the sun dipped from the sky in a blaze of hot color. If he had come to the future to help Katie, he was doing a poor job of it, and he didn't know how to do any better. He couldn't get her cattle back any more than he could prevent a similar theft from happening again. He was at a loss to know how to use his knowledge from the past in the future, but there had to be a way!

The truck stopped by the bunkhouse, and Gus motioned to the door. "You two go on ahead. I'll put the truck away and meet you in the kitchen for supper."

"Right," Travis agreed and climbed out with Mike behind him. Conversation had been at a minimum over the past few hours. Neither he nor the other two men had been able to think of much to say. As Gus drove off, Travis stopped to look across the yard at the house where a single light burned.

"She was pretty upset," Mike said, following Travis's gaze.

"She has a right to be."

Mike shuffled his feet. "I hope this doesn't hurt the ranch."

Travis swung to look at Mike. "What do you mean?"

"Nothing, really," the younger man said. "It's just that things have been tight lately—moneywise, I mean. Ever since Miss Shannon's mother died. Things don't get fixed as quick, supplies are slow being bought. It's just a feeling, but there was talk for a while of her maybe selling the ranch."

"Selling it!"

"Yeah, she and Bill Henry, our old foreman, were meeting a lot in private up at the house before he died. Rumor was the ranch was in trouble, but Bill never said anything and neither did she."

"All ranches go through good times and bad."

"That's what I said!" Mike readily agreed. "And it'll get better. The ranch means a lot to Miss Shannon. She'll take care of it."

"We all will."

"Right. Coming in?" Mike asked, gesturing to the door of the bunkhouse and turning that way.

"In a minute." Mike went inside, and Travis stood for a moment mulling over the young hand's words. If the ranch was in financial trouble, the loss of thirty head of cattle wasn't going to help matters. Slowly Travis turned to walk toward the barn in the growing dusk. The sun had set, and the crickets were coming to life. It was going to be a quiet summer night.

He sighed and shoved his hands into his pockets. As a former lawman, it bothered him that any theft of cattle wasn't going to be reported, but it bothered him more that Katie wanted to do just that but was afraid to. Why? What could reporting the theft to the law do but help her on some chance the stolen cattle were actually found?

Too many questions and not enough answers. If he was going to help Katie, he had to know what was going on. He stopped by the corral to accept the friendly muzzle thrust of a big sorrel gelding. It murmured into his palm before he patted its neck and moved on. Just as he reached the barn and decided to return to the bunkhouse and wait for the morning to talk to Katie about her fears and the ranch's finances, he heard someone talking.

"She's upset but won't call the sheriff."

Travis frowned as he realized someone was on the phone, and the someone was Mark Harrison.

"No, there's nothing that can be done." A pause. "Yes, I'm sure." Another, longer pause. "Tomorrow? I don't see why not. She won't suspect. No one will." The receiver was put back on the hook, and before Travis could move, Mark Harrison stepped outside.

Chapter Eight

"Is there a problem, McCord?" Harrison asked.

"I don't know," Travis answered. "You tell me."

Harrison stiffened at the accusing tone and cast a swift glance back at the door through which he'd just come. His expression was hard to read in the shadow of the Stetson he wore and with the darkness of night settling around them. He shrugged. "No problem. You get that steer and fence taken care of?"

"We did."

Harrison nodded and pulled a pack of cigarettes from his pocket to light one. The brief flare of the lighter illuminated his face. His features were perfectly composed, and no emotion showed in the black of his eyes. He extinguished the flame and exhaled a cloud of smoke. "Something else you wanted, McCord?"

Travis raised a hand to tip his hat back on his head. "I was just wondering how Miss Shannon is."

Harrison's lips twisted into the semblance of a smile. "The lady's fine, McCord, but if you don't believe me, why don't you go check for yourself?"

"Why don't you come with me? You can tell her all about that call you just made."

The smile abruptly left Harrison's face, and deadly silence fell between the two men as they stared at each other. Finally Harrison exhaled another cloud of smoke. "Why don't you mind your own business, McCord?"

"Why don't you want her to know about the call?"

Harrison flicked the cigarette in his hand out into the yard. "McCord, I didn't like it when you got hired. As foreman, I do the hiring and the firing. You might want to remember that." He abruptly swung to walk away toward the kitchen.

Travis frowned as he watched Harrison go. Katie hadn't wanted the theft reported to anybody. She had made it clear that she'd make the only call necessary to a neighboring rancher, but Harrison had purposely disobeyed orders. Why? Travis frowned. The call might have been innocent. Perhaps even requested. What if Simon Griffith was having Harrison keep an eye on Katie and calling him if there was trouble? It was possible.

Across the yard the kitchen door opened and closed as Harrison went inside, and Travis started to walk again. The foreman hadn't acted guilty upon discovering his conversation had been overheard. He hadn't liked being questioned about it, but he hadn't been nervous either. Still, it wouldn't hurt to keep an eye on Harrison and find out exactly what the foreman would be doing and with whom come sunrise.

Suddenly Travis found himself standing in front of the door of the house. He hadn't made a conscious decision to see Katie, but he needed to. Taking off his hat, he knocked. Hurried footsteps followed his rap, and the door abruptly opened.

"Travis!" Surprise was in her voice, but the dark shadow of worry lining her face was quickly erased by the light of unexpected pleasure.

He nodded and twirled the hat in his hand unconsciously. "I wanted to see how you were."

The shadow immediately returned, and her eyes clouded. "I'm fine." But her arms came up in a defensive gesture as she crossed them in front of her. "You needn't have bothered checking."

"It was no bother."

The brilliant blue of his gaze was warm with concern, and the strength of it surprised and touched her. She'd gotten used to dealing with problems and their consequences alone, but Travis had come forward one hundred years in time to make sure she wasn't. But his presence hadn't helped. She was still in trouble. More so than before, but he cared and she needed him to. The night was too black to be alone. She gestured for him to join her. "Please come in."

Silently relieved at her invitation, he stepped inside and turned to watch her close the door behind him.

"You never did get to see the house, did you?" she said, swinging back to take in the hallway with a sweep of her hand. "It's not the same as when Billy built it. A lot of modifications and some additions have been made, but he laid the first foundation." The only lights on in the entire house were in the hallway and in the study, where she'd been when he'd knocked so it was natural to steer him toward the open doors of the room she'd just left. "This was my father's favorite place. It's mine, too."

Travis gave the room a cursory glance, taking in the bookshelves and fireplace, the big desk and stuffed chair, but his attention was centered on Katie as she paced the room, anxiously gesturing and putting on a show of happy bravado.

"He used to work at the desk, and I'd play over here," she said, stopping by an empty space a few feet from some patio doors that looked out on the porch and ranch yard. "My mother used to come in sometimes, too, and we'd all—" She stopped when she turned and found him watching her. "I'm sorry. I'm jabbering."

He watched her nervously brush at her hair. "Why are you afraid, Katie?"

"Afraid? I'm not afraid. I'm...upset." She shrugged and stuffed her hands into the pockets of her jeans. He wanted her to talk about the one subject she wanted to avoid. "It's been a hard day, that's all."

"It's more than the cattle," he persisted, crossing the room to her, but she wouldn't look at him. "I told you I'm here to help."

She swallowed and moved from him to a chair near the fireplace to grasp its back tightly. "There's nothing you can do."

He dropped his hat on a table and slowly came to stand behind her. "How can I know that unless you let me try?"

Her fingers turned white as she clutched at the chair, and she had to blink back the tears that suddenly came to burn her eyes. The urge was strong to turn into his arms where she could find solace against the width of his chest. He could whisper words of reassurance, but his telling her everything would be all right wouldn't make it so. She was on the brink of disaster. "I'm afraid I'm going to lose the ranch."

"Why?"

"Because I don't have any money, that's why!" Angry at the truth, at him for making her tell it, she lashed out. "It's all gone. I had to get a loan from the bank."

He didn't speak but stood silent as she shoved away from the chair and started to pace once more.

"I don't know how it happened." She wrung her hands as she walked. "I don't know why my mother let it happen!"

"You didn't find out until after your mother died that the ranch was in trouble?"

She shook her head. "And we always talked. There wasn't anything about the ranch we didn't discuss. Whenever a problem came up, we worked it out together, but she didn't say anything. I thought everything was fine. But then, after the funeral, the bills started coming." She stopped before the window to push a hand through her hair. "At first I thought it was a mistake. The bills were all legitimate expenses—annual fees, monthly payments—but suddenly everything was past due. Accounts that should have been current were months behind." She spun to face him. "My mother never would have let things go like that!"

"What does Simon say about the bills?"

Katie bit her lip and started to pace again. "He doesn't know about them."

"You didn't tell him?"

She shrugged. "They weren't his responsibility. They were the ranch's. Mine. I asked him after the first few came if my mother had ever said anything about financial problems, but he seemed surprised that I'd asked. I let it drop."

"What about the ranch books?"

She crossed her arms in front of her and continued to walk restlessly. "The last few months before she died, my mother did them." Katie stopped, a puzzled frown pulling at her lips. "It was odd. We used to share the responsibility, but suddenly whenever I offered to help, she turned me down. I didn't understand it, but I didn't question her either. And I should have!"

Travis watched Katie hug herself tightly. "Why? You couldn't have known there was a problem."

"But I should have," she repeated adamantly. "I should have realized something was wrong."

Travis changed the subject. "You didn't see the books for the last few months, but what about anyone else? Your foreman? Simon?"

"No. Bill Henry, our foreman then, knew everything as far as finances, but he never helped with the books."

"And he had no idea there was any problem?"

"None."

"What about Simon? Did he help with the books?"

"No." Katie laughed shortly. "It was a joke, actually. He wanted to help. Seeing as he was so bad at understanding how to operate the ranch, he figured he should at least help with the book work, but my mother wouldn't let him."

"Why?"

"She just didn't feel it was Simon's responsibility. He worked all day at his business. The ranch was hers to look after."

"Did he ever lend your mother any money?"

Katie frowned as she thought back. "No. I don't think he could have even if she'd asked him."

"Why not?"

"I heard my mother and Simon fighting about money a few times. Whenever it happened, I tried to stay discreetly out of the way, but I got the impression that Simon was having trouble."

"Did your mother lend him money?"

"There's nothing in the books to indicate that she did." Katie sighed helplessly. "The books only listed all the bills that hadn't been paid. It was as if my mother had intended to pay them but never wrote the drafts."

"You're sure?"

"If she had, the drafts would have come back from the bank with the monthly statement."

"No drafts were missing?"

Katie shook her head. "No, at least, not that I could tell." And, at his puzzled look, she added, "Right before she died my mother closed one account and opened another, so the drafts currently being drawn on weren't numbered because she hadn't gotten the pre-printed ones from the bank yet."

Travis frowned. "Why did she change the bank account?"

"I wish I knew."

The pain of frustration and misunderstanding echoed in her voice, and Travis's fists clenched at his sides as he watched her from across the room. She seemed weary, lost and without hope, but he had to keep pressing if any answers were to be found. "What about the old ones?"

"All gone. She must have destroyed them."

"No one else could have taken them, done anything with the books after she died?"

"No, there were—are—only two keys to the desk. She kept one. I kept the other."

"Nobody could have found either one and used it when both of you were gone?"

"No, we both always carried the keys with us." She gestured toward the study door. "The house is never locked, but the desk is. All the petty cash and bank records are inside, and keeping the keys with us all the time made it easy to run in the house and get something whenever we needed it rather than rummaging for some hiding place."

Travis turned to look at the desk.

"I used up all the cash reserves to pay off bills," she said and began to circle the room. "But there were so many, and with the usual ranch expenses . . ."

"When did you get the loan?"

Katie's eyes found his. "The week I met you." She looked away again to sigh and gesture expressively. "Simon offered me a loan when he began to suspect I was having trouble, but after hearing the arguments between him and my mother, I didn't want to take the chance of hurting his business while helping the ranch."

"So you went to the bank?"

"Yes. I told them I had a cash flow problem, but I didn't say anything about the debts. It seemed pointless. I'd paid them all." Her footsteps faltered. "Or at least most of them."

"Most?"

Her glance skipped off his. "Some of them I had to just let go. Like the liability insurance for the cattle."

Travis frowned as he tried to comprehend what she meant.

"We were never able to insure every steer we have. It's too expensive. No rancher can do it, but most of the stock was covered." She again crossed her arms in front of her. "But I had to let the insurance lapse. It was too big a bill, and I didn't think it would matter. Not for a few months!"

Understanding dawned. "That's why you didn't want to report the theft to the sheriff."

"I should, I know, but it wouldn't do any good. Not for me. And if the bank finds out..."

Travis watched her struggle with the tears threatening to fall.

"I was going to renew the insurance again before winter but..." She bit a trembling lip. "The loan gives me enough capital to work with, for the usual maintenance and salaries, but it doesn't leave room for any extras. Right now the bank owns more of the ranch than I do. With a good cattle sale this fall, I can pay off most of the loan. It's what the bank's expecting. But if something goes wrong, I won't make it that long and they'll take it from me."

Travis had her in his arms before the first tear slid free, and he hugged her small frame against his tightly. "You're not going to lose the ranch."

Katie trembled at the firm authority in his voice and held on to the words as desperately as she held on to him. "I know. I'm overreacting. We only lost twenty-five, maybe thirty head, not the whole herd."

But those cattle had been meant for the market. He held her close as another tremor shook her.

"I never expected rustlers. They've only come once before. Years ago."

"At the north range, and they never came back."

"Not until now." When she needed every penny the herd could bring. Katie closed her eyes and clung to Travis as if he were an anchor on a stormy sea. Without cash coming in, the ranch couldn't grow. It couldn't expand because she couldn't buy new stock and without new stock, fewer cattle were bred and fewer calves were born. The loan would never be paid off.

Travis recognized the chill of fear. Katie was struggling to hold on to hope when events seemed to be working against her. Her mother had died leaving debts and unanswered questions. A short time later the one person who could help right the wrongs and get the ranch back on its feet died, too. Bill Henry, foreman and friend. Alone Katie was fighting to save the home that had been her family's for generations. She'd lost all cash reserves and was in debt too deep to hope for escape should a catastrophe strike. But why?

Why had Katie's mother suddenly stopped paying bills? What could she have been spending the ranch money on? It didn't make sense that after caring for the Double S for years she would suddenly let the ranch go, any more than it made sense that Katie was continuing to suffer setbacks.

People could be hit by bad luck. It could come in streaks. So could coincidence, but he'd never seen either malady threaten a ranch's existence. Usually that came about from poor management or a bad habit like gambling, but no evidence existed to justify either belief. Someone or something more than bad luck was working against Katie. He just had to find out who or what it was before it was too late.

Katie tried to concentrate on the steady heartbeat beneath her ear instead of on the fear eating at her. The theft of cattle had rocked her, but by itself the loss wasn't permanently damaging. She could still recover and pay off the loan. It would be a little bit harder, and it would take a little bit longer. She just had to be as strong in her beliefs as Travis was. Have faith the way he did.

With his body warming hers, she wondered how he could be so sure, so strong for her when he had to be overwhelmed by his own circumstances. One hundred years separated them, but he'd crossed them all to reach her. She lifted her head to stare up at him and found him waiting for her.

With his hands framing her face, Travis watched a soft flush brush her cheeks as his thumbs gently wiped away the tracks of her tears. "You're not going to lose the ranch."

A smile trembled across her lips as her eyes searched his. "I'm going to do my best not to." It was hard to concentrate on talking with his legs pressed against hers and the muscles of his back moving against her palms. She moistened her lips only to have his eyes fasten on her mouth. "I'm being emotional."

He smiled at her breathless excuse.

"I hope you don't mind."

His head lowered toward hers. "Not at all."

Her eyes closed as his lips claimed hers, but even expecting the embrace, she wasn't prepared for the explosion of sensation that came with his kiss. Her stomach flipped, her blood raced and her head swam. His fingers left a trail of heat as his hands moved down her arms to her back where their imprint burned through her thin cotton T-shirt and into her skin.

Never had a woman melted in his arms before. Katie was like liquid fire. Her mouth melded with his, her body molded perfectly to the contours of his own and her legs seemed to be part of his. With slow deliberation he let his hands slide down her back only to rise again as her breasts yielded against the solid width of his chest. Even through the cotton of her shirt he could feel the heat of her flesh responding to his touch, and the jolt of desire that shot through him when she moved against him caused exquisite pain.

She murmured as their lips slowly parted, but their faces stayed close. The blazing blue of his eyes stared down into hers, and she stretched up to rub her mouth against his. Before he could respond to the taunt, she pulled away slightly to run her hands from his waist up to the hard line of his shoulders. "Travis."

The word was no more than a murmur. His mouth dropped to plunder hers, and she gave herself in wild abandon. Her fingers curled into his hair and pulled his head farther downward, but as she pressed forward, her feet suddenly left the floor.

With a startled laugh she broke away as he lifted her to his eye level. She wrapped her arms around his neck and felt his hands slide from her waist to fold her against him. Her buttocks were cushioned against his forearms as he cradled her. She smiled at the control the position gave her. With his hands otherwise occupied, he was hers for the taking. She leaned forward and blew in his ear.

He shuddered and watched gold light dance in the warm brown of her eyes as she began exploring his face with her eyes and lips. Half of him wanted to drop and ravage her on the spot, but the other half resisted the urge, wanting to enjoy the sweet torment she was administering.

Nuzzling, kissing, tasting, she teased and trembled as she remained firmly against his chest. Beneath her hands the muscles of his shoulders bunched at the effort of holding her high, but there was no evidence of strain in the blue of his eyes. His gaze held only silent laughter as he watched her indulge in a freedom she had never before experienced.

She had been kissed by other men, and she had kissed them back. But never had she been the one to lead the way while her partner stood still. She had followed the pace, not set it. She'd never thought or wanted to do otherwise. Being in control now was a heady sensation. It gave her the courage to nip and tuck when with others she would have cut and run.

Travis caught Katie's lips with his own as she tried to draw away, and pulled her back. She was driving him insane with her gentle touches and little caresses. He wanted to use his hands to copy her motions with some of his own, but he was loath to let her down. He didn't want to wipe away the shy smile on her lips, the uncertain but daring light in her eyes. Yet suddenly his hands were freed when her legs lifted to circle his body in a tight embrace.

Katie gasped as the demands of his mouth were abruptly matched by those of his hands. His fingers and palms traced her back, her arms, and tangled in her hair. With a pounding heart she realized the situation was getting out of hand, but she didn't care. Unfortunately, Travis did.

In his time, dalliances with a lady weren't taken lightly. Not all ladies had deserved respect, and more than a few had crossed the line beyond flirtation and given up virtue before a promise was given. He didn't condemn them for their actions, but he wasn't about to compromise Katie. He wanted to give her more, take more, but the only thing he could provide for certain was her safety. Until he knew he could give beyond that, until he knew her future was secure and that his tomorrow could permanently blend with hers, it was selfish to attempt more. Reluctantly he drew back to rest his forehead against hers. His breathing was heavy. "I should go."

She shook her head, but before she could protest he released her, setting her down to stand on a stool before him.

His eyes clung to hers. Even time hadn't prepared him for Katie Shannon. No woman had ever responded as openly and uniquely as she had, and he'd never wanted to give back as much or more than he got.

Katie pulled her gaze from his. "You can stay—"

"No." His hand lifted to brush her hair back from her face. "Not yet. Not until I know I can."

Cold fear shook her as he stepped back and reached for his hat. "Travis?" She put out a hand to stop him, but he was already walking away. Hastily she followed him to the door and caught his arm. "What do you mean?"

He avoided her eyes. "The future." He shook his head. He didn't know what his future was, what it could be. He hadn't given much thought to his tomorrow. Only Katie's—until, suddenly, he wanted his to be part of hers and not for just a short time.

She threw her arms around him. "You can't leave."

"I don't want to."

She trembled against him. She couldn't imagine a life without Travis. "You told me that you'd come here for me."

"I did."

"But?"

He shook his head. "I don't know how long I can stay."

She leaned back to gaze up at him, her fingers curling into his shirt. "Why? I don't understand."

"I'm supposed to be dead." He put a finger across her lips when she tried to object. "When I've done what I'm supposed to—"

She broke away from his restraining hand. "No! You can't go back! You can't leave until I tell you that you can!"

He smiled at her fierce declaration and reached out to cup her cheek. "I'm here for as long as you need me."

She covered his hand with her own. "Then you're not going anywhere for a long time."

He grinned. "No, ma'am," he agreed and brought her back to him for a draining kiss, but the embrace didn't last. He put her from him. "Dinner's getting cold."

His hands left her and it was all Katie could do to keep standing, especially when the look in his eyes told her food wasn't what he wanted to eat, but then the door closed behind him and he was gone.

Chapter Nine

Travis shifted in the saddle and lifted a hand to remove his hat, using the sleeve of his shirt to wipe the sweat from his forehead. He, Mike and some of the other hands were scouring the west range trying to regather the stock that had been scattered by the rustlers. It was hot, tedious work.

Tilting his head back to squint up at the sun, Travis redonned the Stetson and turned his attention back to the half-dozen head he'd flushed out of hiding and was driving toward the main herd. The time hadn't come to send the beef to market yet but it wouldn't be much longer, and Katie needed every steer that could be found.

His lips curved into a smile as she came to mind. A little woman she might be but a lot of female was packed into her body, and all the curves were in the right places.

"Yo, Travis!"

He turned in the saddle to find Mike heading his way driving about the same number of head he had before him. "Mike! Good hunting?"

"Great! We should have the herd back together by the end of the day."

The two men came to ride side by side as the cattle mixed and plodded on, breaking through some brush and coming in sight of the herd. Among the men sitting a horse by the gathering stock was Mark Harrison.

Travis frowned. The "tomorrow" of Harrison's conversation appeared to be harmless enough. Whoever he'd been speaking to, the call could have done no more than confirm the loss and acknowledge the regathering of the stock the next day, but what was it that Katie, or anyone else, wouldn't "suspect"?

Ushering the steers in with the rest, Travis and Mike pulled up beside Gus, who was sitting his mustang on the opposite side of the herd from Harrison. The older hand nodded and gestured to the cattle. "It's looking good. Better than I had hoped."

"I told Travis that we might just be done by sunset."

"Maybe," Gus agreed, "but the boss says the three of us are going to be baby-sitting this herd tonight and sweeping the area again tomorrow."

"But we can't be missing more than half a dozen!" Mike protested. "Having three men search for six lost steers a dozen men can't find is a waste of time!"

"Maybe Harrison's thinking the rustlers might come back," Travis offered.

"Not likely," Gus said, turning to spit into the dirt. "Chances are they'd get caught once everyone's alerted."

"Except no one's been told about the rustlers but Ed Peck who runs cattle to the south of us," Travis objected.

"The rustlers don't know that," Gus denied with an adamant shake of his head. "Beats me why they would have come to the west range instead of the north. The north end is easier to get to."

"Probably because the stock hadn't been moved there yet," Mike answered. "They just got settled up yonder yesterday."

Travis's gaze sharpened on Mike, but Gus just grunted. "You're right. Forgot about that." He nodded toward the milling steers. "You two better head back out again. The boss is watching."

Travis moved off with Mike, remaining silent until they were well away from the herd. "You knew Bill Henry?"

"Yes. Good man, good foreman. He'd been ramroding this outfit for years before Harrison."

"Killed in a car accident?"

"Yeah, his truck went off the road one night on the way back from Hancock. It was raining and dark. Sheriff figured he just lost control."

"Bad luck."

Mike grunted ready agreement. "For everyone."

"Where did Harrison come from?"

"Don't know exactly. He doesn't talk about himself much." Mike grimaced. "But I guess Miss Shannon got his name from somebody who recommended him."

Travis nodded thoughtfully. "You here when her mother died?"

"Bad luck there, too," Mike said with a shake of his head. "A few months before Bill Henry was killed she went out riding alone, and her horse must have thrown her. Spooked or something. She hit her head when she fell." Mike's eyebrows met in a line beneath the rim of his Stetson. "And Mrs. Shannon was a good rider."

Travis frowned in surprise. Katie had never said, but he'd assumed her mother had died of natural causes. His eyes darkened. Two accidental deaths in such a short time seemed a bit coincidental. "Why did she keep going by Mrs. Shannon rather than Griffith?"

Mike gave a guilty grimace. "That was more us than her. We'd called her Mrs. Shannon for so long it was hard to get used to calling her anything else—especially when we hardly ever saw her new husband."

"Simon didn't do anything with the ranch?"

Mike grinned. "Couldn't barely ride a horse, but he was a good sport about it. He asked a lot of questions when he first came, but you could tell he just didn't understand. He's a city slicker clear through. Can't tell a stallion from a mare or a Hereford from an Angus." Mike's grin broadened. "First time he went out to the range, he asked to see the longhorns."

Travis returned the grin. Longhorn cattle could still be found on many ranches, but for good beef, the Herefords and other breeds had been brought in long before he'd become sheriff of Eagle River.

"You could see Mr. Griffith leave every morning and come home every night about the same time. My mom said he was a typical businessman. Whatever that is. But he was good to Mrs. Shannon. Used to bring her roses from town all the time. Real romantic. Thought I'd try that when I get to town again."

"You do that, Mike, and I'll bring some red ones to your wedding."

The younger man flushed. "Geez, who said anything about getting married?"

Travis laughed and looked around them. The herd was far behind, and it was time to split up. "How long would it take to get to the north range from here?"

"An hour, maybe more, why?"

"I thought I'd try going skunk hunting tonight."

"Skunk hunting?" Mike questioned. "But Harrison wants us to stay with the herd."

"Gus'll be here."

The grin returned to Mike's face. The idea of disobeying the new foreman had appeal. "Harrison should be leaving soon. He'll take his truck and go back to the house to see Miss Shannon. We can leave the horse trailer here and take our truck out the other way. He'll never know."

"Not unless you tell him."

A FEW HOURS LATER, Mike glanced across the seat to Travis, who sat in the passenger seat examining a carbine. They were in the truck heading north. Gus had remained behind at the line shack. When they'd told him their plan, he'd just shaken his head. He had no great respect for the new Double S foreman either. "Know how to use that?"

"I've been known to hit a target or two," Travis answered, not taking his eyes or his hands off the rifle. He would have preferred to have his Colt handy as well as the rifle, but the six-shooter was back in the bunkhouse. He stroked the weapon in his hands. It was smooth and light and promised a clean shot on an easy trigger. If they headed into trouble, the rifle would serve his purpose well. "What about you?"

"Used to go rabbit hunting as a kid. Can't recall shooting any skunk before, though."

"Maybe we won't find any, but I have a hunch we will." A wild hunch. One he almost hoped wouldn't pay off. "You know where the herd is gathered?"

"Just about."

"Think you can pull in around there, nice and easy without anyone seeing us?" Trying to sneak up on someone in a machine that made a lot of noise wasn't something he'd attempted before.

Mike threw him a puzzled look. "Who's going to be there to see us?"

"The skunks."

Mike laughed. "McCord, you are definitely missing a few."

"A few what?"

Mike's laughter filled the cab as he slowed the truck and turned off to the side below a ridge. "Okay, Sheriff McCord, lawman of Eagle River, the herd's over the rise. You want we should sneak up on them?"

"That's the plan." Travis stepped out of the truck and looked to the sky. The sun was almost down, and Gus had said this was a likely time for rustlers to strike. Any ranch hands would be gone for the day. The cattle would be alone and unguarded, but it would still be light enough for any would-be thieves to see where they were going and what they were doing.

Mike followed Travis out of the cab. "How are we going to see any skunks in the dark? I thought we'd use the headlights."

"If I'm right, we won't need them." Travis headed up the rise with the rifle in his hands.

A baffled Mike followed with a carbine of his own, but the question he was about to ask died on his lips when he hit the top and looked down. "Look at that!"

Travis reached up and grabbed Mike to pull him down to his knees beside him, but he never looked away from the cattle or the truck being pulled in close to them.

In the headlights of the big semi, the cattle shifted and bawled uneasily. Behind the truck, deep tire tracks were cut into the ground off to the north. The fence was a mile off, but it had no doubt been cut to let the truck through from the highway beyond.

As Travis and Mike watched, the truck stopped and some men climbed from the cab. "Three men," Travis counted as the trio moved to the back of the truck to let down the gate.

"What are we going to do?" Mike asked in a hushed whisper.

"Stop them."

"How?" Mike's eyes widened as Travis cocked the rifle he held. The game they were getting ready to hunt wasn't the kind Mike had thought they'd be chasing. Swallowing tightly, he cocked his own weapon and looked back to the rustlers.

A smile touched Travis's mouth as he glanced at a sober Mike. He had little doubt the young cowhand had never shot at a human before, but Mike was ready to do what he had to. Thieves were stealing his boss's cattle, and protecting what belonged to the Double S came with the job. "First we have to get closer." But as he started to stand, a motor coughed to life, and he watched a small three-wheeled vehicle rumble down the ramp of the truck. "What is that?"

"An all-terrain bike. They're probably going to use it to round up the cattle."

Travis shook his head and longed for the simplicity of a horse and saddle. "You go left. I'll go right. Get close but stay out of sight."

"What then?"

"Follow my lead."

Mike licked dry lips and nodded. "Don't take too long."

Travis moved off into the brush on the other side of the ridge and down onto the rugged meadow where the stock had been put to graze. The ground was rough and rolling. It had good grass for grazing, but it also had a lot of cover. He used it to creep amidst the herd and closer to the truck, all the time watching the three-wheeled vehicle buzz around in efficient circles to move the animals in the direction of the waiting ramp. The one headlight on the handle bars of the machine groped toward the steers in the growing darkness, and Travis dropped to his stomach as the rider steadily drew closer to his position.

Beyond the cattle, the other thieves waited by the truck. The headlights of the big semi had been left on to illuminate the work in the meadow, and the two men were silhouetted against the beams. One of them had a long-nosed rifle in his hand. Travis nodded as he watched the men from his cover. He'd expected a fight.

The sound of the motor drew closer, and Travis got to his knees behind a gouge in the land. He'd knocked men from horses before while on the ground, but from an all-terrain vehicle? He braced himself. The hum of the engine grew louder, the shaft of light from the headlight bounced over the land, and the vehicle came at him out of the settling dusk.

For a moment Travis was caught and held in the glare of the light as he stepped into the vehicle's path. The rider cried out in surprise, twisted the handlebars to avoid a collision, but was too late to dodge the rifle.

The carbine slammed into his chest. The rider tumbled over backward out of the seat, and the bike careened madly onward without its driver.

Travis leapt aside as someone yelled, and a bullet sang. He hit the dirt beside the fallen rider, ready to use the rifle as a club again, but there was no need. Unconscious and sprawled across the grass, the rustler lay on his back with his eyes closed.

"One down, two to go," Travis muttered and rolled away as another shot sounded, but it wasn't aimed at him. It was coming from his left. Mike. An answering bullet followed from the semi, and the two remaining men ran out of the headlights to take cover in the night.

Travis fired with Mike, trying to pin down the rustlers, but it didn't take long for the two thieves to realize they didn't want to stay. One man lurched for the cab of the truck as the other continued to fire. As cattle bawled and milled wildly around him, Travis concentrated on the man with the gun. Putting his rifle to his shoulder, he took careful aim on the flash from the outlaw's weapon and fired.

The man cried out, and the truck's motor roared to life. From the left Travis saw Mike jump up. "He's getting away!"

Before Travis could react, Mike started to run, firing as he went. It was the last straw for the cattle. A joint bellow came from the scattered steers, and Travis yelled, "Stampede!"

The herd wasn't running in mass, but ducking and swinging in between small groups of the frightened animals kept both men from shooting at the semi that had started backing up.

In vain Travis watched the retreating vehicle. How could he stop it? A horse could be shot from under a man if need be, but what good would shooting the truck do?

"The tires! Hit the tires!"

Stumbling away from a charging steer, Travis responded to Mike's cry and aimed and fired. It didn't seem to have an effect, but he kept shooting until he was sure he'd hit every tire he could see and his gun was empty. When he stopped, though, Mike was still shooting. As the bullets flew, the windshield cracked and a headlight popped. Abruptly the brakes on the truck hissed, the driver's door flew open and a man jumped out to disappear into the darkness.

"He got away."

Travis looked from where the thief had run to where Mike stood a short distance away. Miraculously neither Mike nor he had been touched by the cattle that had charged across the meadow. "He won't get far on foot."

Moving cautiously forward together, Travis and Mike reloaded their guns and approached the man Travis had shot. Travis knelt beside the prone figure and put a hand to the man's neck.

"Is he dead?" Mike asked, his stomach rolling uneasily. It was difficult to see much with the sun down, but the remaining headlight of the truck illuminated enough that he could see the blood.

Travis stood. "Afraid so." He glanced back at the meadow. "There's a live one out there."

"We better go get him."

Travis nodded, but a quick glance at the truck stopped him. All the tires were flat. A grin spread across his mouth at the sight. The machines might be bigger and faster, but just like a wagon, they couldn't roll without a wheel.

"SKUNK HUNTING?" the deputy sheriff asked and glanced from Mike to Travis. "You two were skunk hunting?"

The meadow was alive with lights and sound. One squad car sat by the disabled semi. Another was parked at the edge of the field. Both had red lights flashing across the scene, and both had their head-lights pointing into the black of night that lay across the land.

Other vehicles were also scattered around. Mike had run back to the pickup and its radio once the remaining rustler had been tied and had called for help before driving the truck to the meadow to wait with Travis. It had taken an hour before anyone'd shown up, but the first group to arrive had rapidly been followed by others, among them a pickup from the ranch carrying Katie, Simon and Mark Harrison.

Looking past the sheriff, Travis watched Katie as she stood speaking with another uniformed officer with Harrison beside her. She looked dazed, confused, and Travis wanted to go to her. He'd barely been able to say a word to her since she'd come.

She'd gotten to the meadow at almost the same time as the first squad car. Everyone had wanted answers at once, and the man wearing the star had gotten to ask questions first.

Travis had let Mike do most of the talking and had followed his lead when Mike continued with the excuse of skunk hunting. Mike didn't really understand how a hunch had brought Travis to the conclusion that rustlers would be at the north range, and skunk hunting was a lot easier to explain than a feeling he hadn't shared.

"Dangedest thing I ever heard," the deputy muttered and shut the notebook in his hand. "But it's a good thing you decided to go hunting or your boss would have been minus some beef."

"Job security, officer." Mike beamed, his thumbs looped into the waistband of his denims. The rifles he and Travis had used were back in the ranch pickup and out of sight at the request of the deputies. The only weapons to be seen were the guns all the lawmen had on their hips—a tradition Travis was glad to see continue. When a man was enforcing the law, he never knew when he'd need more than a word or a fist to keep someone in line.

"You shot the dead man?"

"Seemed the thing to do with him shooting at me," Travis answered as he looked up to see Katie standing nearby waiting for him. His stomach tightened at the fear he saw in her eyes.

"He clobbered the other one, too," Mike put in. "I got the truck."

The deputy grinned. "We're going to have to get a mechanic out here tomorrow to put some new tires on so we can roll this thing out of here." He looked to Travis again. "You new to these parts?"

Alarm had Katie stepping forward. How could Travis explain his presence? What could he possibly say about his being on the ranch? "He just started working here a few weeks ago," she answered before Travis could speak. "Is there a problem?"

"No," the deputy assured her. "No one's going to blame him for shooting in self-defense—or even if he wasn't, considering he was firing at rustlers." He looked at Travis. "I wouldn't plan on leaving the county for a while, though."

"I'm not going anywhere." His eyes were on Katie as he spoke, and a smile tugged at his lips. Thinking he was in need, she'd come to his rescue.

The deputy put his hand to the hat he wore and nodded to Katie. "I think you can all go back to the ranch now. If we have any more questions, we'll come out tomorrow."

"Thank you." Katie watched him walk back to join one of the other deputies before turning to look at Travis and Mike.

"Guess I know how we're going to be spending tomorrow," Mike said with a heartfelt sigh. "Finding the cattle that just stampeded halfway to the Mexican border." Shoving his hands into his pockets, he walked away toward some of the other ranch hands.

"He's a good man," Travis said as Mike went. "Didn't flinch once he knew what needed to be done."

Suddenly furious, Katie glared up at him. "Travis, this isn't 1883, and you're not the sheriff anymore. You could both have been hurt."

Travis met the dark concern in her eyes. "We weren't."

She looked away, her hands stuffed into the pockets of the jacket she wore to protect herself from the cool night air. She shivered anyway. It would have been bad enough to lose more cattle, but to lose Travis... "I can't believe they came back again."

"They won't be back anymore."

"No." One was dead, one was on his way to jail and the other, who had escaped on foot, would hopefully be in custody shortly.

Travis stared down at her bent head, fighting the urge to reach out and touch her, but too many people were standing nearby and he didn't know how she'd react to the gesture. She wasn't supposed to be anything more to him than his boss. That she had become much more was something he hadn't expected. "Are you all right?"

"Because of you I am."

When she lifted her head he could see tears in her eyes, and a wealth of emotion he wasn't prepared to receive. The breath caught in his throat. "Glad I could help."

She smiled, and when his hand came up to brush her cheek, her fingers caught his. Any lingering doubts about his being from the past, about his being who he said he was, were evaporating rapidly. It was getting harder and harder not to believe him. Her smile trembled. "You're really good at this sort of thing, aren't you? It's no wonder they made you sheriff of Eagle River."

He grinned. "That may have had something to do with it, but I have to admit I never had to try to catch anyone on a motorized all-terrain vehicle before. I think it was easier when rustlers just used horses."

Katie laughed, a rich sound that echoed across the meadow, and she stepped forward to give him a hug. A million questions were buzzing in her head about the past, the present, the future. Belief was making her dizzy. "I don't know how you got here or why, Travis McCord, but I do know I'm glad you came."

He returned the hug. "Happy to oblige, ma'am." His attention was drawn from her as the red lights from one of the squad cars were turned off and it started to move away. "Come on. It's late, and it's cold out with the sun down. We had all best get back to the ranch.''

Katie turned with Travis, his arm across her shoulders, but they'd taken only a few steps when she saw Mark Harrison coming toward them. She glanced up at Travis. Her questions would have to wait. "I think Mark wants to talk to you."

"That's all right. I want to talk to him, too."

She frowned at the suppressed anger in his voice, but when the ranch foreman stopped before them, she reluctantly moved on to leave the two men alone.

"Nice piece of work," Harrison told Travis. The headlights from the remaining vehicles were casting sharp shadows across his face under the rim of his hat. "But I'd like to know how the two of you got up here when you're supposed to be out on the west end of the ranch."

"Just following up on your phone call."

Harrison stood very still. "What's that supposed to mean?"

"You tell me. You were talking to someone about the stock and about today being all right, as I recall."

A seemingly incredulous grin twisted Harrison's face. "You think I had something to do with the rustlers coming here?"

"I think the rustlers had to know where the stock was in order to steal it. This herd was brought in yesterday. The steers on the west range had been there only a day when the rustlers came. How would they know when and where to hit unless someone was telling them?"

"And you're accusing me?" Harrison jerked his thumb over his shoulder at the departing squad car. "Anyone on the ranch could have told someone where the stock's being held, but if you're so certain I'm the one, why don't you turn me in to the sheriff?"

"Because I don't have any proof. Yet."

"Yeah, well, you know what I think, McCord? I think that job as sheriff of Eagle River has given you delusions of grandeur. Until you can prove otherwise, you're not a cop, and I'm not a thief. You're a ranch hand and I'm the foreman, and I don't like ranch hands who disobey orders." Harrison's finger hit Travis hard in the chest. "From now on when I tell you to go somewhere, you stay there until I tell you to leave. You were lucky tonight. Your hero act saved you your job. Next time you get out of line you're going to be back in your ghost town sweeping up spiderwebs."

Harrison spun on his heel, but Travis stopped him. "Want to know what I think?"

Harrison's fists clenched as he whirled around to face Travis.

"I think, if you know anything about the rustling, from now on the ranch is going to be a very dangerous place to be."

"Is that a threat, McCord?"

"No, a fact."

Engines started as the other vehicles began pulling away, and Mike came back from the other ranch hands, oblivious to the tension locking his friend and the Double S foreman together. "Miss Shannon's ready to go if we are. She's waiting in the truck."

Harrison broke the stare first, glancing at Mike before looking again at Travis. "You two best get back where you belong."

Mike groaned when Harrison was out of earshot. "We've got to go all the way back to the line shack?"

"Someone's going to have to tell Gus what happened," Travis answered, not looking away from Harrison's retreating back.

"Hey, yeah!" Mike agreed enthusiastically, suddenly not tired anymore. "Let's go."

Travis followed Mike slowly, watching Harrison step inside the pickup cab with Katie and Simon before moving himself. He didn't know for sure if Harrison was involved in any of the goings-on at the ranch. No proof existed to say he was. The phone call had sounded suspicious, but that the rustlers had come to take the cattle on the day Harrison had been speaking of could have been coincidence. Stranger things had happened, and the law said a man was innocent until proven guilty.

Still, if he was behind the stealing, knowing someone was watching him would make Harrison think twice before trying something else. It might even give him motivation to move along to some other job if he carried any blame. Travis pulled open the truck door and stepped inside. Having caught the rustlers, he felt better. One hundred years hadn't taken away his ability to protect. It made him that much more certain he could help Katie if he stayed on. And it confirmed she was why time had shifted. He'd come into the future for her. But once his job was done, would time let him stay with her?

Chapter Ten

News of the rustlers, the rescue and the ensuing gun battle traveled quickly once dawn came. The ranch buzzed with it, and so did the town of Hancock. Phone lines were humming as everyone tried to find out all the details, and Katie found her doorbell ringing with annoying regularity as well.

It pleased her that so many people were concerned, but the interest the rustling was generating was making it nearly impossible to get anything done. And it worried her that some overenthusiastic reporter would start looking into Travis's past. Frowning, she set the phone back in the cradle once more and picked up her pencil, only to have the doorbell go off again.

With an angry sigh she shoved herself away from the desk and, muttering under her breath, crossed the room to the hall and the front door where she was met by the beaming smile of a short, balding man she knew too well. Tom Risley from the *Hancock Chronicle*.

"Katie, how are you this morning?" he asked, brimming with congeniality and solicitous concern. But then, a reporter had to know how to win friends and influence people.

"Fine, Tom," she returned, crossing her arms in front of her and barricading the door with all five foot two of her less-than-bulky frame. Smile or not, friend or not, he wasn't getting past her or she'd never get him out of the house. His poking around would only waste her time and possibly endanger Travis.

"I imagine you know why I'm here."

Katie smiled, too, but didn't budge. "I imagine I do."

"I'd like to talk to the two hometown heroes."

"Hometown... Travis isn't from Hancock."

"He is now." Tom pointed down the steps to a car where another man sat. "Helena even sent someone out to see them. Seems your two hands are going to be famous."

Katie bit her lip. Fame was going to rocket Travis into the headlines unless she could stop it, and that wasn't going to be easy.

"You were out there, too, I hear." He took her arm and drew her out of the house before she could stop him. "It's important that we get everyone's story."

"But what about the sheriff—"

"Already talked to him and the deputies. They wouldn't let us talk to the rustler, though." Risley motioned to the other man. "Phil Harper, this is Katie Shannon. She owns the Double S."

Before the man could grasp her hand Katie spotted her foreman and called for help. "Mark!" She smiled at Risley and Harper. "Travis and Mike are out working the range, but Mark Harrison, my foreman, was there. He can tell you all about what happened." She took a step backward toward the house.

Harrison came forward, tipping his hat to Katie, accepting handshakes from the two men and warding off questions at the same time. "Yes, I was there with Miss Shannon. We got there just as the sheriff arrived."

A diplomatic retreat seemed possible and proper, but Katie didn't get two steps away before Risley had her by the elbow and had her trapped. Yet it was Travis and Mike the two newsmen were after, and as if on cue, their battered pickup pulled into the yard.

"Here they are now," Mark said, and the two reporters were gone before the words were out of his mouth.

Fear closed Katie's throat, and her desire to disappear into the quiet of the study vanished as she saw Travis step out of the pickup and into the sunlight. She didn't want him talking to reporters, getting his picture in the paper and becoming a local celebrity. It wasn't safe. And, he belonged to her. Yet as she watched Risley and Harper advance on him, Travis didn't seem worried by their presence. Frowning, she bit her lip and wondered. Was it possible that she was overreacting? Being selfish? If Travis had managed to overcome the differences of one hundred years enough to maintain a job and lead a productive life, did he really need her to protect him?

She continued to watch as, confronted by two jabbering strangers with pens and paper, tape recorders and cameras, Travis just relaxed and stayed with them. Mike, on the other hand, was all motion. His arms waved, his mouth smiled and he bounced from side to side as he repeated the night's events in vivid detail.

Katie couldn't stop the grin that tugged at her mouth. Mike obviously was going to enjoy playing the hero to the hilt. Travis, on the other hand, was accepting the interest as if it was part of his job. She sighed. She supposed being sheriff of Eagle River had made him a target for newsmen whenever something happened. She shook her head. From where she was standing, her man from the past didn't need her help in dealing with those from the future. She glanced at Harrison and was surprised to find his eyes black with resentment. "Problem, Mark?"

"McCord might be."

"How so?"

"He wasn't where he was supposed to be last night. Neither was Gardine."

"And it's a good thing they weren't," Katie objected. "Otherwise we'd have lost more cattle."

"They disobeyed orders."

"And I hope you told them to watch it in the future, but in this instance, I don't think more than a word of warning is necessary."

Harrison turned away from watching the reporters and the Double S men. "Gardine wouldn't have left the line shack if it hadn't been for McCord. McCord's a bad influence."

Katie frowned. "Have any of the men complained about him or his work?"

"Not yet."

She shook her head. "Don't look for something that isn't there, Mark. And don't expect him to be perfect. Travis McCord is just a man. He'll make mistakes just as you and I do."

"Maybe."

Harrison strode away, and Katie watched him go with troubled eyes. Not for the first time she wondered if she'd made a mistake in hiring someone from outside the ranch as her foreman, even if Mark had come well recommended.

Turning to go back to the house, she paused to look once more at Travis and Mike as they talked with the reporters, but the sound of a motor and the crunch of tires on the dirt road leading to the ranch yard had her turning around again. A black sports car was coming, and she bit her lip as she recognized it. Ken was back.

Ken Baxter was a nice-looking man who had proven to be a lot of fun to spend time with. And, at least at first, it had been exciting to have a man asking her to dances or movies or dinner, but the enthusiasm she'd had for seeing him had begun to wane once the initial glitter had worn off and she'd realized the two of them had nothing in common.

Ken loved the city, fast cars, fancy clothes and winning. He liked to impress and tended to brag, and yet he had a sensitive side that appealed. When not caught up in relating some story or another, he was an excellent listener and a caring friend. He had excellent taste in music and food, was a wonderful suitor who brought flowers and gifts, but he didn't like the ranch.

In many ways her relationship with Ken reminded Katie of that of her mother and Simon. Opposites who had attracted. They had appeared to be happy, but her mother and Simon had never meshed completely. The lack of common ground had somehow managed to keep them apart. Love hadn't been quite enough to make the ranch house a home to Simon, and he had never become the companion Katie felt her mother had been seeking. The ranch had kept David and Pauline Shannon together, but it had held Simon and Pauline apart.

As Katie watched Ken come toward her, she was struck more by their differences than their similari-

ties. Her mother had liked Ken. Simon did, too. But
was liking enough? Her gaze drifted across the yard to
the battered pickup and the men by it. It had been until Travis had come.

"Katie!"

Swept into a warm embrace, she returned his hug
and accepted his kiss with a smile, but she didn't linger in his arms. "Ken, I wasn't expecting you."

His hands stayed on her shoulders. "I came as soon
as I could. When I heard about the rustlers—are you
all right?"

She laughed. "Of course I am."

Ken drew her back against him. "When Simon
called to tell me what happened out here last night
while he was visiting, I was worried. I've been trying
to reach you all morning."

"You and half the town of Hancock." She pulled
out of his arms to take his hand and led him away
from the house and toward the barn. Going inside to
the study with Ken would only remind her of what had
happened when she'd been there last with Travis.

"Simon told me this wasn't the first theft."

"No, but it will be the last." Her gaze drifted across
the yard to Travis. He had come from the past for her,
to help her, and he had. A chill shook her. But would
he stay once he'd fulfilled what he saw as his purpose? He had a past and a present, but he didn't know
if he could have a future.

She glanced up at Ken. "You shouldn't have been
worried. It wasn't as dramatic as the old Western
movies make it. It was over in a matter of a few minutes."

"But a man was killed!"

Katie nodded, pulling her hand from his as she pushed open the barn door. "Yes, and one got away, but we didn't lose any cattle."

She stepped inside, and Ken followed. He gestured to the building above and around them. "This damn ranch, Katie. It worries me."

She stopped by a stall where a pregnant mare stood, nose outstretched. "Why?"

"Because it hurts you!"

"Ken—"

"This place is too big for you to handle. All the problems running it entail, the jumbling of figures, the constant dealing with men you barely know, the stress, the worry. You don't need it!"

"This is my home," she retorted calmly, but anger was near.

"And you love it, I know, but don't you see, Katie, you'll never be able to hang on to it. Why don't you let it go now while you have all the good memories? Don't let it drag you down!"

Ken reached for her, but Katie pulled away. "I am not going to give up. Things aren't that bad."

"Not yet." He stared down at her. "Simon told me about the loan."

Katie gritted her teeth. "He had no business telling you anything."

Ken looked wounded. "He's worried about you. He knows I am, too." Ken stepped forward to put his hands on her shoulders. "Katie, there's nothing wrong with admitting you can't win."

She glared silently up at him.

"Why are you being so stubborn when you could sell this place and marry me? With the money we

could buy a nice home of our own in the city and enjoy ourselves.''

Katie met his pleading gray eyes with a steady stare.
"What do you want more, Ken? Me or the money
from the ranch?''

He blinked as if she'd slapped him, and his hands
dropped to his sides. "How can you say that?''

"Ever since my mother's death that's all you've told
me. Sell the ranch. Sell the ranch. When are you going to understand that I don't want to sell the ranch?''
She paced away from him. "This is my home, and I'm
going to stay here until someone forces me out!''

"Like rustlers?''

Katie spun to face him. "Travis and Mike stopped
the rustlers.''

"Yes, Travis McCord, the alleged sheriff of Eagle
River.'' Ken shook his head. "Perhaps you don't know
that he's been lying to you.''

Her heart stopped. "What do you mean?''

"He was never hired to guard Eagle River,'' Ken
told her. "He was never hired by anyone to do anything as far as I can find.''

"You've had him investigated?'' Katie asked, her
stomach sinking in alarm.

"Yes, and he doesn't exist.''

"That's ridiculous,'' she retorted but swung away
to hide her fear. "Besides, I knew about Eagle River.''

"You knew he was lying, and you still hired him?''
Katie turned to face him. "He's a good hand.''

"By whose standards? Not your foreman's.''

"Mark doesn't like Travis—or anyone else, for that
matter,'' she snapped back, crossing her arms in front
of her. "He's the one I'm sorry I hired.''

Ken gestured dramatically. "I can't believe what I'm hearing. This Travis McCord is turning you against everyone you know!" Ken caught her by the arms. "You accuse me of looking for your money, but what about him? Sounds to me like he's kissing up to the boss!"

"You don't know what you're talking about!"

"Don't I? Isn't it interesting that he just happened to be where the rustlers were in time to stop them? A man without a past suddenly appears to save the day."

"Are you accusing Travis of being involved in the rustling?" she demanded incredulously.

"Why else would he have been where he wasn't supposed to be?"

"I was there because no one else believed the rustlers would strike twice."

"Travis!" Katie swung and found him standing at the end of the barn. "Travis!"

As he stepped forward slowly to within a few feet of Ken, silent rage and speculation burned in Travis. Having stood still for the reporters, satisfied their need for pictures and words, he'd come to the barn and for the past several minutes had been listening to Katie argue with Baxter. He hadn't wanted to eavesdrop. He hadn't even wanted to go to the barn, but he hadn't been able to help himself.

When he'd seen Katie in Baxter's arms, gut-wrenching jealousy had nearly sent him across the yard. He'd wanted to plant his fist in Baxter's smiling face, but instead he'd stayed with the reporters and watched Katie walk off alone with the man. She'd seemed happy enough with her hand in his, but the sight had done little to please Travis. Envy had driven him to follow them, but anger was what had made him speak.

"Nobody could understand why the rustlers had hit the west range when the north range was so much easier to get to by truck, but the cattle hadn't been moved to the north range until a couple days ago." Travis stared hard at Ken. "I went there following a blind hunch, and it paid off."

"You told everyone that you were skunk hunting!" Ken said in distaste. "You were really out looking for glory."

"I was out looking to stop some thieves if they came," Travis countered evenly and turned to Katie. "I could have told someone else, but if I'd been wrong, people wouldn't have been too happy."

"But now you're a hero," Ken countered.

"I'm not a hero. I'm just a ranch hand."

"Your modesty is touching."

"You're out of line, Ken," Katie interrupted. "I think you'd better leave."

Ken glared at Travis, then turned to her. "Don't you see what he's doing, Katie?"

"He's helping me keep the ranch."

"That's only what he wants you to think!"

Katie put a hand to her head. "Ken, this has gone far enough. Thank you for coming to see me, but your worry is unnecessary. I'm fine. The rustlers didn't hurt me, and they didn't hurt the ranch."

Ken glared at her before swinging away to stride to the door. "You're going to regret this."

Katie listened as angry footsteps carried him away before turning to one of the stalls to rest her forehead against the upper bar. When Travis stopped beside her, she didn't look up. "He wants me to sell the ranch."

"I heard."

"Then you heard about everything." She pulled back to meet his steady gaze. "Seems you always get to see Ken at his worst."

Travis shrugged and leaned against the stall wall. "Jealousy does strange things to a man." He'd just found that out for himself.

"You're too kind," Katie told him. "Ken's more concerned about himself than me. He doesn't need me."

"He wants you."

"Needing and wanting aren't the same." She'd wanted Ken, at least for a while, but she needed Travis. She turned to face him. "He had you investigated. He didn't find anything, but the reporters—"

"Won't find anything, either. I'm just a boy from Abilene."

"Abilene." She knew so little about him and wanted to know so much more. She should have asked before. Could have. There'd been time. Opportunity. Over the past weeks the common bond of love for the past had brought them closer together. Yet with all the storytelling, the sharing, she'd never asked him to share himself. Perhaps she'd been afraid to. Hearing more would have forced her to admit he was telling the truth when she hadn't yet been ready to believe. And now that she did believe, he was talking about leaving. Fear threatened to close her throat. "Tell me. Tell me about you."

The desperation in her voice touched him, and he knew its cause. The uncertain future. If he did what he was supposed to, freed her from whoever or whatever was trying to hurt her, would he go to the grave he was supposed to be in? Or would he be set free to live again?

She was in his arms it seemed without taking a step. The distance just closed between them, and they were together. Her fingers tangled in his hair and dragged his head down.

The fierceness of the embrace shook him. The deepness of it touched him. Catching and holding her close, he was overwhelmed once more with how small in size she was but how much power she had to lure him. Her lips were a temptation he had to taste, her body a prize he had to touch, but even as he got what he desired, he cursed his own weakness at giving in to her.

Trembling against him, she clung to his shoulders. The way they kept coming together, without warning, without words, made her believe he was as helpless as she against the tide that swept them into each other's arms.

Travis pulled back, watching as her eyes fluttered open to gaze up at him. Never before had he lost control with a woman, but with Katie, it was a possibility. Slowly he let his grip slacken, and she slipped back down onto her feet from where she'd stood stretched up against him on her toes. "Kissing the boss is getting to be a habit."

She trembled again at the gravelly note in his voice, knowing she had put it there, and flushed. "If the boss would stop throwing herself at you, maybe that wouldn't happen."

"It takes two to tangle."

Unconsciously she licked her lips and watched his attention focus on her action. She hadn't meant to bait him, but nonetheless she felt the muscles of his arms tighten around her. He drew her forward, and her legs wrapped around one of his thighs. She opened her mouth to protest. Someone could come into the barn at any moment. They could be caught, and the gossip would be merciless. Yet it was difficult to care when she saw his head dip again toward hers.

"Here comes the chopper!" The call came from just outside the door, and it startled Katie.

She jumped against Travis and swung her head to listen as the steady thump of a motor grew louder. "It must be Ed."

Travis frowned at the increasing noise. He'd never heard anything like it before. A roar accompanied by what sounded like hundreds of wings beating the air. He started to tighten his grip on Katie, but she was suddenly out of his arms and pulling him toward the door.

"Come on! You can meet him!"

Travis stepped outside into a storm of gathering wind and dust and raised startled eyes to watch a machine drop out of the sky. His heart skipped into his throat as he saw metal blades whirling and realized Katie was running straight toward them.

The machine touched down, and Katie waved to the man who stepped from it. He waved back and came toward her. Ed Peck was of medium height, fifty and carried more weight around his middle than he had when he was younger, but he had a good heart and a laugh that was as contagious as it was loud. "Ed!"

"Katie!" he yelled over the racket, and took her arm to lead her farther away from the wind and noise of the helicopter.

Having stopped several feet back, Travis stared in mute awe at the machine that could fly. A helicopter. He'd read about them and about airplanes and such.

Mike came to stand beside Travis with Gus. "You're white as a sheet!" he shouted as the din died down with the cutting of the engine.

"Haven't you ever seen a whirlybird before, Travis?" Gus asked with a grin.

"Whirlybird?" Travis repeated, still staring at the massive machine of glass and metal. No wheels adorned this vehicle. It didn't roll like a wagon. It really flew like a bird!

"Helicopter!" Mike clarified and slapped Travis on the back. "I swear, Travis, sometimes I think you came from another century or something."

"Helicopter," Travis said, letting the word roll off his tongue. Seeing a picture of one in a book wasn't anything like seeing one up close. Wonder helped him swallow his fear. "You actually round up cattle with that thing?"

"We do!" Ed Peck said, coming forward with Katie. "A lot easier than doing it in a saddle." He laughed and everyone laughed with him, responding to the booming sound of his good humor and the warmth of his personality. Only Travis remained silent and sober. Staring at the middle-aged man with dancing blue eyes as if he was crazy, Travis tried to imagine someone preferring to ride in the noisy "whirlybird" than on a horse.

"This is Travis McCord, Ed," Katie said. "You already know Gus and Mike."

"So this is the other hero!" Ed exclaimed and reached out to take Travis's hand in a firm grip. "Nice job. You, too, Mike, but what's this bull about skunk hunting?"

Laughter rang again as everyone looked to Travis, including Mike, who was prepared to let him have the spotlight for a while. "Seemed like a good idea at the time," Travis responded with a shrug.

Ed gave another bark of laughter. "You caught the skunks, at any rate, and for that we're all thankful. Saved Katie here another loss that no rancher needs." He looked at her. "I didn't hear any talk about the other hit by the rustlers on the west end."

Katie shrugged under his steady stare. Without her saying anything, Travis and Mike and even Mark had kept the prior theft from the sheriff. "Banks and insurance companies don't like to hear about losses."

Ed grunted. "You lose many?"

"Near as we can tell, maybe thirty head," she answered.

Ed shook his head. "Bad enough, but how about roundup? You almost ready to go?"

Katie nodded. "Almost."

"Want to go up to take a look at what we've got?"

"You can take Travis," Mike volunteered.

Katie grinned at the petrified look that came to Travis's face. It was customary for her to take her foreman, but she didn't see Mark anywhere. He'd disappeared after the reporters had come, probably to the north end to see how the stock gathering was coming. "Why not?"

Ed clapped Travis on the shoulder, recognizing the fear of flying in the blue of Travis's eyes. "I'll guarantee a ride you won't forget."

Mike gave Travis a shove, and Katie took his arm. "Come on, cowboy."

Travis was tempted to cut and run but couldn't get past the curiosity that was carrying his feet forward. He barely heard Ed describe the machine as they climbed inside, and once the engine was started, it was impossible to hear anything at all. His hands were shaking as Katie showed him how to strap himself into the seat beside her and gave him a headset like those he'd seen in the library. He put them over his ears and looked forward to the front seats where the pilot and Ed sat talking and making hand signals. It took a moment before Travis realized that he could hear them over the headset, and when he did, he sent Katie an elated grin.

The helicopter took to the sky, but as Katie watched Travis, she knew the butterflies in her stomach had little to do with the lift-off. He was like a child, eager to try and do and see. He shone with the wonder of learning something new and exciting.

Smiling silently, she sat back in her seat and studied him as he looked out the window. With his innocence, honesty and devastating masculinity, he was a man like none other. And, by his own admission, he was all hers.

Chapter Eleven

When the accidents started to happen, Travis didn't suspect anything at first. It wasn't unusual for saddle cinches to snap or for ropes to break, and when objects fell, gravity didn't care if someone was standing where what was falling was doomed to land. But, while those things happened only occasionally to everyone else, he suddenly found them happening to him a lot. It didn't take much deduction for him to realize that somebody wanted him out of the way.

He tried to identify someone who was always around when the accidents happened, but it was impossible. A saddle cinch could be tampered with during broad daylight or in the dead of night. The same for a rope, or another piece of equipment. Whoever was trying to get to him only had to know where he'd be working or what he'd be doing on a given day to attempt a setup, and everyone on the ranch knew who was going to be where doing what most of the time.

Stopping to wipe the sweat from his forehead, Travis sighed in frustration and looked down from the hayloft where he was working. That someone was after him meant someone was still after Katie, but who? Grimly he surveyed the ranch yard beyond the barn from the loft doors. He had no answers, but at least as long as he was the target, Katie would be left alone.

"All set!"

Travis waved acknowledgment to Mike, who was standing directly below the loft in the back of a tractor trailer loaded with hay. Like himself, Mike was stripped to the waist in the summer heat. The only thing he wore on his upper body was a pair of gloves and his hat.

After spending the past few days at the old homestead with a few other men working the range, moving stock and checking fences, they'd been relegated to ranch yard duty. It was their turn to unload and store the freshly harvested and bound bales of hay.

Travis started pulling on the rope in his hands. The whole operation consisted of two men, two ropes and a pulley. One rope ran from a hook to the ground. The other ran from a hook to the loft. The man on the ground used his rope and the pulley to lift the bale to the hayloft doors. The man in the loft used his rope to pull the bale from where it hung outside into the loft. When Travis got hold of the bale and heaved it onto a waiting stack, he returned to the open loft doors to motion down to Mike. "You about ready to take a turn up here?"

Mike wiped the sweat from his upper lip with a bare forearm and nodded. "I don't know what's worse. Pulling the hay from the ground up or standing up there in the heat piling the bales."

Travis grinned. "Mean you'd rather be out riding a horse than doing this?"

Mike groaned. "Great time for the conveyor to break down." Usually hoisting the bales one at a time into the loft was unnecessary. The ranch had a machine with a conveyor belt that carried the hay from the ground to the loft. The men had only to put the bales on the belt and take them off again when the hay reached the loft. But the machine had broken down late the day before, and the repairman had yet to arrive to fix it.

"Maybe Harrison's right. I'm a jinx." All the accidents had made him the butt of many a joke, and he was relentlessly teased about having slippery fingers, being accident-prone or, as the foreman put it, being a jinx.

Mike rolled his eyes and readjusted his Stetson. "When he told you to try not to break anything this morning, you should have reminded him the conveyor was already broken before you started working in the loft."

"Thought I'd save my breath." Harrison didn't need much of an excuse to lay out more harassment.

"What'd you ever do to him to make him like you so much, anyway?" Mike asked.

"Got a job without his permission." Travis grabbed the rope and stepped onto the hook. "I'll let myself down. Why don't you head for the ladder?"

Mike jumped to the ground from the trailer with a silent wave and disappeared inside the shadows of the barn below while Travis swung out the window and, hand over hand, lowered himself from the loft to the yard by standing on the hook.

Coming out of the kitchen, Katie stopped to watch him jump from the ground onto the waiting trailer. In no time he had a bale hooked and was using the rope and pulley to lift the hay up to Mike in the loft. The strain of the work had every muscle in his chest and arms flexing, and the power of his movements was mesmerizing.

The sun played across the lean length of his naked back and stroked the broad width of his shoulders. Perspiration coated his skin and dampened the dark hair on his chest and arms. She couldn't see an ounce of fat on him. Travis was hard and strong, but even if his hands were callused beneath the gloves he wore, his touch was soft. Gentle. When he held her in his arms she felt as fragile as a flower, and if he ever left, she'd wilt like one.

Katie bit her lip. She'd fallen in love with her man from the past and she wanted to believe the feeling was mutual, but Travis wasn't confessing his feelings. He was keeping them to himself and resisting any talk of the future. Or the possibility of his lack of one. Suppressing a shiver, she left the shade of the porch where Travis couldn't see her and stepped out into the sunlight.

Travis didn't know Katie was coming. His back was to her, and her approach was silent. But he knew she was there. When Mike got hold of the bale just lifted, Travis turned from the rope to find her standing by the trailer, and a sensation he couldn't describe shot through his body. Yet he understood the heat that came with it and knew the cause wasn't the sun beating down on him. He stooped to bring himself closer to eye level, though the trailer still kept him above her, and watched a soft flush of pleasure fill her face as his gaze met hers. To him it seemed years had passed, rather than days, since he'd held her against him. "Hi."

The one word took all the strength out of her knees. She had to put her hands on the trailer to stop from sinking to the ground. "You're almost done?" she asked, silently wishing Mike wasn't in the loft above them. Travis smelled of sweat and hay, and she wanted desperately to reach out and touch the warm expanse of his exposed skin.

"This load." He gestured to the barn. "You here to check on Annabelle?"

Katie smiled. The mare had given birth to a beautiful filly the day before. "I want to see how they're doing."

While she answered his question, Travis had a hard time following her words. To be so close without being able to touch her was agony, but his policy had always been business before pleasure. He had to do what he'd come for. He wasn't going to let Katie down as he had Molly. Or maybe his purpose was only an excuse. With Katie, not only was he out of his time, he was out of his depth. No woman had ever held him in her spell before, and it was like stepping into a trap. Yet he didn't want to escape. He wanted to stay. He wanted a future.

When he didn't speak, Katie licked suddenly dry lips to look up at Mike. "The repairman should be here by noon," she called up to him. "Maybe if the two of you quit early to have lunch, he'll have the conveyor fixed by then."

Mike grinned as he sent the hook back down to Travis who easily caught it and sank it into another bale. "Sounds good to me. I won't mind letting a machine do the work."

Travis started pulling on the rope, and Katie took the cue to step away from the trailer and start toward the barn.

When the bale reached the loft, Travis lowered his gaze to watch her go. He'd been thinking a lot about her lately and about the financial problems she was experiencing with the ranch. Even his dreams involved money. Money in the form of Tyler Fenton's gold. Travis frowned as he tried again to grasp and hold on to the visions of the old miner, but he couldn't understand whatever it was that Tyler was trying to tell him.

An unexpected snap from above had Travis looking upward. In the space of a heartbeat he saw Mike's petrified face, watched him give a terrified jerk on the line that nearly dragged him out the loft doors, and saw the bale start to fall. A glance was all it took to tell him where it was going to land—on top of Katie!

Looking up at the loud pop, she frowned as the rope dropped away, and the bale stopped to hover over her in midair. Puzzled by the lack of motion, she frowned, but then, abruptly, the hay started to fall. A strangled cry locked in her throat and she tried to move, but her limbs froze. Her feet were glued to the ground. She put up her hands to ward off the blow and was suddenly hit from behind.

Travis tackled and carried her forward into the dirt. The bale followed them.

Crashing to earth, the hay landed with an echoing thud mere inches from Travis's legs. The impact sent a billowing cloud of dust into the air.

Travis coughed as it filled his lungs, but his thoughts were only for Katie. Grabbing her by the shoulders, he turned her over to stare down into her face. "Are you all right?"

Dazed and winded, she choked on the dirt whirling around them and managed a nod as Mike came racing out of the barn.

His face was white. He didn't even think he'd touched any of the rungs on his way down the ladder. "I tried to stop it. I—"

Travis held up a hand to silence him and helped Katie to her feet. "We're fine. Just a bit dirty." He studied her face to make sure there was no sign of pain or injury, but there were only tears caused by the dust making her eyes water. As he watched, her gaze shifted from him to the bale lying nearby.

"I checked the rope this morning, Miss Shannon. I swear I did," Mike told her, following her startled stare. "Right before breakfast I stopped to make sure it hadn't gotten worn through yesterday."

"I know you did," Travis assured him. "I saw you do it."

Katie glanced away from the bale and up to Travis. She would have been crushed. "I—"

"What's going on here?" The three turned to find Mark Harrison bearing down on them. His face was set, his eyes black with fury. "What the hell happened?"

"The rope broke," Mike answered lamely and glanced down at his hands to see them shaking. It had been close. Too damn close.

Harrison immediately looked to Travis. "You again. Seems you can't touch anything lately without breaking it."

"Mark—" Katie began, but Travis swung to confront her foreman. He'd had enough. If someone wanted to try to hurt or maim him, that was one thing, but injuring Katie was another.

"Maybe that's because someone wants it to be that way," Travis told him. "Like you."

The accusation made Harrison's mouth thin even more than it already was. "That's it, McCord! You're out of here! You're fired! I want you off this ranch!"

Katie quickly put herself between the two men. "Mark! Travis! Stop it! It was an accident!"

"He's no accident!" Harrison thundered. "He's been making trouble since he came, and I want him out of here." He reached out and shoved Katie aside. It was the wrong thing to do.

Travis exploded. He threw his arm back and swung.

Harrison staggered back from the blow but didn't even stop to put a hand up to feel the blood on his chin. He charged. Harrison slammed into Travis, and the two men spun backward into the barn.

Watching, Katie stood in openmouthed surprise as fists flailed and grunts filled the air. It took a moment for her to find her voice. "Stop it!" Her demand did no good. If the men had heard her, they ignored her command. She stamped her foot. "Travis! Mark! Stop it right now!" But the words fell on deaf ears. The two weren't ready or willing to listen to her. Travis's head snapped back as Harrison landed a punch, and she swung on Mike in helpless desperation. "Do something!"

Faced with her unexpected demand, the grin left Mike's face. He'd been enjoying the fight. Ever since Mark Harrison had come to the Double S, Mike had been wishing someone would put their knuckles in his face, but now that somebody was finally doing it, the boss didn't like it. "Yes, ma'am!" He stepped forward to intercept the struggling men but stopped when he realized to get in between them was to become a victim of their blows. He turned back to Katie. "How?"

Travis sank his fist into Harrison's abdomen and heard the air hiss from the man's lips, but the foreman was by no means beaten. Harrison was equal in size and weight, and he was hard, too. Physical labor had seen both of them toughened against labor and abuse. Harrison swung back.

Travis blocked the blow and was immediately hit with a blast of water. He ducked and spun, but the water followed him briefly before hitting and stopping Harrison.

"Now will you both stop?"

Dripping and bleeding, Travis turned to find Katie. With her hands on her hips, she was glaring at him while Mike stood beside her manning a hose. Travis grinned, but Harrison's sense of humor had taken a beating.

With a split lip, sore ribs and a bloody nose, he swung toward Travis. "I want him out of here!"

Travis looked from Katie to Harrison before bending to retrieve the Stetson he'd lost during the battle. There wasn't anything he could say. He'd hit the ranch foreman. If not for the interruption, he'd still be hitting him. He ran a hand through his dripping hair before putting on his hat. Whatever the punishment was, he deserved it.

"You never should have hired him without asking me!" Harrison continued, whirling toward Katie. He'd lost his hat during the fight, too, and water was running down his face and soaking his shirt.

Katie looked from one man to the other. Travis wouldn't meet her eyes. He was looking at the ground. Ashamed for fighting? But he'd only swung to defend her. She turned to her foreman. "Mark, let's everyone calm down." She glanced back up at the pulley above her and then down to the bale of hay that could have taken her life. "We're all upset—"

"He goes or I go!" Harrison roared, reached down to grab his Stetson and slapped it on his head.

"Mark—"

"You have a choice."

Katie stared at him. He was her foreman. He was supposed to be helping her, but instead he was giving ultimatums. She took a deep breath. "No one has to go, Mark."

"Are you saying he's not fired?"

"Mark, Travis isn't going to leave because of what happened here," she told him.

"Then I am." Harrison turned and strode away, his back stiff and his steps angry.

Katie knew she should go after him. He was her foreman. She needed him. Her hand raised, but she immediately let it drop.

"I'm sorry."

She looked up to find Travis beside her. "I'm not. I never liked him."

Travis grinned. "Me neither."

"Yes!" They both turned to watch Mike do a jig as he turned the hose on himself.

"Mike," Travis said, "why don't you turn off the hose and go get a new rope?"

With water running down his face and chest, Mike just grinned. "Be right back." He swung away with the hose.

Travis pointed after him. "You think of the hose?"

"No, he did. Mumbled something about it always working on fighting cats and dogs." The smile on her lips faded as she looked away from Mike's retreating figure to Travis. "You're bleeding."

Her hand touched his face, and he caught it to let her lead him into the barn and the first aid kit kept on a shelf by the doors. He grinned as she opened it and stepped onto a stool. The movement brought her up to his height.

"Come here," she told him, her face all business as she took a piece of gauze from the box. He did as he was told, and she gently reached up to dab at his bloody nose with one hand while using the other to firmly hold his chin in place. She searched his face as she worked. A few scrapes, some discoloration. She frowned. "I don't see any other blood. Do you hurt anywhere else?"

The only pain he was conscious of had nothing to do with the fight. The throb of his ribs where hard knuckles had hit was easily forgotten when the sweet scent of her was filling his senses. Travis's eyes dropped to her throat and moved down to the movements of the white T-shirt over her breasts. "No."

The deep tone of the response made her gaze fly to his, and her breath caught when she found him watching her with raw hunger. His hands settled on her hips, and he drew her forward. "Travis." Her hands dropped to his bare shoulders, the gauze clutched in her fist forgotten.

"Kiss me, Katie."

"Mike . . ."

"Isn't here." Travis's lips covered hers, and he felt her sag against him.

The gauze left her fingers to fall to the floor as she gripped the hard width of his shoulders. She could feel muscle flexing. Her palms followed the motions down over the hard bulge of his biceps, and when his hands slid from her hips to her back, she slipped her fingers between their bodies to run them up his rib cage. Cold water, warm sweat, but his skin was hot. His flesh burned her, while the soft hairs covering his chest teased.

Sweet torment. Her inquisitive touch was igniting a fire. It licked at the pit of his stomach. She murmured against his lips as his head dropped and he tasted her throat with his tongue.

Trembling, she felt his hands cup her buttocks to press her hips to his. She could feel his want. It matched her need. She clung to him, oblivious to the shadow that fell across the door.

Mike stopped in his tracks when he saw them. Travis and the boss were entangled together like a sculpture of living art. The first aid kit was beside them on a stall wall. A piece of gauze lay on the floor. It was the first time Mike had ever seen mouth-to-mouth resuscitation being given to a man with a bloody nose. Discreetly he backed out of the barn.

Katie found herself looking into blue eyes blazing with passion. The fire in Travis was about to consume her, and she didn't care. She lifted her mouth to his.

"Travis! Where are you?"

Both Katie and Travis froze at the call. "Mike," Travis said and suppressed the shudder threatening to overtake him. Taking a deep breath, he had to force himself to let go of her, but her fingers remained glued to his flesh.

She didn't want him to stop. She was ready to let him quench the answering fire he'd ignited in her even if it meant his ravishing her in the hay on the barn floor. The realization brought embarrassed heat to her face and shame to her core. Desperate not to lose him, wanting to secure a future with him, she was ready to throw even her dignity aside. Her hands and eyes dropped from him. "I have to go."

Before he could stop her, Katie was out the door. Travis stood, dazed at her sudden absence.

"You okay?"

Travis turned to find Mike watching him. "Fine. Got the rope?"

"Yup, but it looks like you got your hands full, too."

Travis's eyes sharpened on Mike, but there was no mocking smirk on the younger man's face. Travis sighed. "Yeah."

"You like her?"

"Too much."

Mike watched Travis retrieve the discarded piece of gauze from the floor before closing the first aid kit and replacing it on the shelf. "You want to marry her?"

The thought brought Travis up short, but a warm feeling spread through him at the idea. "Funny, I never thought I was the marrying kind."

"You could do worse. So could she." Mike made a face. "You're a lot better than Baxter."

Travis laughed and reached out to take the rope. "I think that's a compliment. Come on, let's get going." But as he followed Mike outside, his thoughts were troubled. Marrying Katie. He'd actually managed to fall in love with the woman he'd come forward in time to save. Yet he felt no joy at confronting his emotions, only the agony of uncertainty. He was not only out of *his* time, but perhaps out of time completely. If the past was really waiting to take him back, if the grave he belonged in was waiting to be filled, his love for her would be something he could only briefly experience.

The afternoon passed, the sun set and Travis returned with Mike to the bunkhouse after dinner. Doubts continued to plague him. He wanted to go to Katie, talk to her. Though the past had brought them together, the future stood between them. He sat on his bunk. Somehow they had to reach an understanding, find a way to live with whatever lay beyond the morrow.

Outside Katie crossed the yard to the barn with the blanket of night wrapped around her. She never had seen Annabelle earlier. The mare and her filly had been forgotten when Travis had once again taken her into his arms.

Several horses nickered as she closed the door behind her and turned on the lights overhead, and curious heads came out of stalls to look at her as she walked down the aisle to the mare. Annabelle met her with an inquisitive murmur, but as Katie petted the affectionate sorrel, her thoughts went to Travis. It was agony to be with him yet apart from him, not knowing if he could stay, or if he would go.

Letting herself into the stall, she didn't hear the rustling sounds at the back of the barn or see any movement in the shadows. Unaware, she sank to the floor to admire the long-legged foal that stood on wobbly legs nursing, but her joy in observing new life was fleeting.

Closing her eyes, she leaned back against the stall wall and stroked the tawny fur of one of the barn cats that quickly came to find a place in her lap. A smile curved her lips as the familiar scents of the barn soothed and surrounded her and the cat purred in loud contentment. As a little girl she had often crept off to the barn to sit. It seemed she had always loved the smell of the hay and the earth and all the animals, and convincing her parents to let her sleep in the loft was something she had been quite good at.

Abruptly the cat bolted from her lap, and Katie opened her eyes to watch the big tabby jump to the top of the stall to stare toward the back of the barn. Its tail jerked in silent agitation, and Katie frowned and listened. She didn't hear anything unusual.

Getting to her feet, she reached out to pet the tabby to try to reassure it, but the cat suddenly leapt from the stall and ran down the aisle and out of the barn. Behind her the sorrel mare unexpectedly pulled away from the foal to nicker uncertainly, and down the way a hoof banged against wood as the other horses in the barn started to stir.

Katie hastily let herself out of the stall and stood in the aisle, trying to see or hear what was disturbing the stock. A wild animal could have gotten inside. Yet it wasn't what she saw or heard that alarmed her. It was what she smelled. Something was burning!

Running toward the back of the barn, she gasped at the deadly shadows of dancing flames. "No!"

Panicked cries from the animals echoed her own, and as she ran to grab a fire extinguisher from a nearby beam and hit the alarm, anxious hooves began pawing at stall doors.

Smoke clogged her lungs and burned her eyes as she raced to fight the flames, but try as she might, the fire extinguisher was no match for the blaze that had erupted in the newly stacked hay. Flames were licking greedily on either side of the aisle and were racing across the floor. If the fire reached the wall, the entire building would go!

A sudden burst of fresh air came in through the open back door, and Katie turned in time to see some burning hay land on the bale next to her. Before she could move, the bundle ignited, and flames shot upward. She screamed and jumped aside, falling to the floor.

"Katie!"

She looked over her shoulder at the call, and suddenly Travis was holding her. "The horses! We have to save the horses!"

Frantically running from stall to stall, they flung open doors, and terrified animals stampeded outside, where other ranch hands were arriving. Annabelle and her foal were the last stall Travis reached, and he waved the mare out with her wobbly-kneed filly. He grabbed Katie's hand. "Come on!"

Reluctant to go, she pulled free of his grip at the door to turn and stare at the barn. The flames were crawling up the walls, dancing wildly across the floor and eagerly consuming all in their path. The building was lost.

Travis grabbed her again as Gus and some of the other hands turned hoses on the barn and tried to herd the horses into a nearby corral. He yanked her into a run.

Katie stumbled after him until he'd dragged her across the yard. When he stopped, it was to take her by the shoulders and shake her.

"You stay here!"

She had no chance to reply before he dashed off to help the others.

The ranch hands fought to beat the all-consuming inferno. Travis led them in a race they were determined to win. Together, wrestling with buckets and hoses, the men tried to be quick, but the fire beat them back. Helpless against a merciless enemy, Travis stumbled back with the others, away from the heat and smoke, and stared at the burning building. It was useless. The fire had too good a hold. The fresh hay was just what the flames needed to stay alive. The barn couldn't be saved. The alarm, still ringing in the yard, had come too late. Standing beside Gus, he watched the structure start to collapse.

"How could this happen?" Gus asked, his face stained with soot and smoke.

Travis's jaw clenched. The fire was no accident. It had been planned. Someone had waited until the barn was full of fresh hay to set it. He turned from Gus to find Katie, but when he saw her, his heart wrenched inside his chest.

When the alarm had gone off, he'd almost been to the barn. A few quick steps and he'd been at the door and seen the flames. In that dreadful instant he'd been sure she was trapped, but it wasn't death that had her locked in its grip. It was defeat.

Standing where he'd left her, she was staring at the barn. Tears stained her cheeks, and black ash was smudged across her skin and clothing. The angry reflection of the flames danced in her eyes, and the pain of the fire's victory lined her face.

Slowly he walked toward her, but it was a long time before she turned away from the destruction to him.

Stunned, Katie stared up at Travis. She couldn't believe what was happening. It seemed a dream. A nightmare. Across the yard flames were devouring her last chance. "It's over," she finally told him. "Gone. I've lost it all."

Travis reached for her as a broken sob caught in her throat, and he held her in helpless rage until the barn collapsed and she could cry no more.

Chapter Twelve

Katie sat at the desk, chin in hand, staring at its empty top. It was pointless to go over the books again. She wasn't going to find any mathematical error to tell her the ranch was running in the plus rather than in the minus.

Sitting back in the big leather chair, she looked at the clock, calmly ticking time away over the fireplace. It was early yet. It would be a few hours before the bank opened. She bit her lip. How soon would they hear the news about the barn? She should probably call and tell them herself, but why rush the inevitable? If she waited, maybe it would be Monday before the axe would fall.

She closed her eyes. Sleep was something that had eluded her during the night. Once the barn had collapsed, Helen had led her up to the house, fed her some brandy and sent her to bed while Travis and the men watched the ashes to insure the fire had died. But being in bed hadn't encouraged her to rest. Rather, she'd lain staring at the ceiling until dawn had come to touch the sky. It wasn't that she had been overwrought or that she'd been busy thinking. She hadn't been doing anything. Still wasn't. She wasn't tired, she wasn't angry, she wasn't anything. Except, maybe, empty.

She supposed it was shock making her feel so numb. Or, maybe it was just relief. The worry was over. She opened her eyes again and stared at the phone on the desk. Was Travis awake yet? She turned away from the instrument. It wasn't that she had anything in particular to say to him. She just wanted to hear his voice, but what could he say? He'd come forward in time to help her, but one man hadn't been enough to overcome the demons of fate that were determined to take the ranch from her.

"Aren't you ready to go yet?"

Katie looked up at the question and blinked when she found Travis standing in the doorway. Had her thoughts brought him to her? Showered and changed, gone was the clothing blackened by fire. He was dressed in clean jeans and a fresh shirt, and he was wearing his wonderful smile. Only this time the expression didn't affect her. While her heart jumped at his unexpected presence, she could muster no enthusiasm to respond to him. With losing the ranch, she'd lost him, too. No more boss, no more ranch, no more purpose for him to remain with her. And, if he left, that meant she'd lose everything. "Go where?"

Travis pushed the Stetson back on his head. She looked small and alone and lost. He wanted to go to her and pull her into his arms, but she didn't need his comfort. She needed his help, and he had only one more chance to give it. "To Tyler Fenton's place."

She frowned. "Why?"

"To look for gold."

She sighed. "Travis, I can't go anywhere. I've got to stay here and call the bank."

"What for?"

"Travis . . ."

He strode across the room to the chair and pulled her to her feet. At least she was up and dressed. He'd been afraid he'd have to haul her out of bed. "Come on."

With her hand trapped in his, she didn't have much choice but to follow, but she didn't go willingly. "Travis, this is no time for games. I know you mean well and I'm sure you're trying to cheer me up, but—"

"Gold will cheer you up."

They reached the front door, and she planted her feet firmly on the floor to bring him to a halt. "Travis, I said no!"

"Okay." He dropped her hand and, in one swift motion, bent and threw her over his shoulder.

"Travis!" The world turned upside down as he carried her outside and down the steps. "Put me down!"

"Got it all ready?" she heard Travis ask, and was suddenly back on the ground standing between him and Mike.

Mike grinned and gestured to the truck and trailer beside them. "Ready to go. The horses are in back."

"Travis, what—?"

He opened the door and hoisted her inside behind the wheel. "You'd better drive. You're better at it than I am." He slammed the door and turned to Mike. "Anyone asks, you tell them we're out looking for gold."

Mike waved and backed away as Travis jogged around the truck to get in the cab on the passenger side.

Katie watched him climb in and close the door. "Travis—"

"Would you rather be doing this or calling the bank?"

She met the openness of his stare with a troubled frown. What he was suggesting was ridiculous. She couldn't run away from her troubles. On the other hand, they'd still be there when she came back. "I don't want to call the bank."

He grinned. "So drive, Miss Shannon. Daylight's a-wasting."

A reluctant smile twisted her lips. "Okay, Sheriff McCord. Whatever you say."

The drive out to the broken-down buildings Tyler Fenton had once lived in was quiet. Though the sky was gray above with impending rain clouds and the outlook for her future was far from bright, somehow the pain of losing her home wasn't as harsh with Travis beside her. She glanced at him as they neared their destination and felt her throat tighten with emotion. He was still trying to give her hope—even if it was only through a ridiculous side trip into the past.

"Better not park too close to the front door," Travis said as the buildings came into view. "Tyler never liked people blocking his view."

Katie rolled her eyes as she pulled the truck to a stop, but before she could comment, Travis was out the door.

Going to the trailer and releasing the gate, he was whistling and feeling happier and more confident than he had in a long time. All the other trips he'd made to the past with Katie had been sad and seemingly without hope, but that wasn't how he felt anymore. And he wasn't going to let her feel that way either.

She joined him at the back of the trailer and watched him guide the two horses out. Both were saddled and ready to ride. "We're searching for gold on horseback?" she asked.

He threw her a grin as he stepped forward to check her horse's saddle cinch. "Trust me." And at her doubting look, he stopped what he was doing and took her by the arms. "I know where Tyler's gold is."

Her jaw dropped open in surprise. "Travis!"

"I've been thinking about it, and something's been nagging at me. Something I saw, something Tyler said. He had gold, Katie. I never believed it then, but I do now. And I think I know where to find it."

She studied his face and saw only earnest appeal in his eyes. Was it possible?

"Help me, Katie. I know it's out there." He squeezed her shoulders in reassurance before releasing her and reaching up into the saddlebags of his waiting horse to pull out his holster and the Colt. "It's been a few years, you know. Things have probably changed over by the stream, but we can do it if we work together."

She met his gaze. Whether pipe dream or reality, she couldn't resist his plea. "Which way do we go?"

In moments they were mounted, and he was leading her from the truck, past the dilapidated house and barn and over a long-forgotten footpath to the ridge beyond. He took her down by the stream and looked around him. "It was near here that I stumbled on Tyler one day. I caught him by surprise, and he got overly flustered."

Katie chewed at her lip. "As if he was hiding something?"

Travis nodded. "He was dirty, as if he'd been digging, but he didn't have any pans or picks with him, and a man doesn't go hunting gold with his bare hands."

"You think he was hiding his gold."

Travis nodded and pointed to the bank and the ridge beyond. "Tyler was on this side of the creek when I saw him so let's look here. You go upstream, and I'll go down."

"What am I looking for?"

"A hiding place. A cave, maybe." Travis didn't see her move to begin the search, but he knew she would and he knew he was right. Having gone over and over again the scene that day when he'd come upon Tyler by the stream, he was certain Tyler had been hiding something, and the only thing of value Tyler'd had to hide was gold. He must have stumbled upon Tyler just after the old miner had left his cache of gold.

After an hour, though, they had no results, and Katie's faith was getting shaky as it started to rain. "Travis, there's nothing here."

"You're wrong," he insisted, urging his horse across the water to hers. "It's here somewhere." He gestured around them. "This is where Tyler panned for gold, and it's where he hid it. Rather than lugging it back to the shack where someone else might find it when he was out digging, he kept it here where he spent most of his time."

Katie frowned as she considered. "But it's been so long, Travis."

"It's still here. I know it."

Wanting to believe him, Katie looked around her. "Are you sure he didn't bury it somewhere rather than just hiding it?"

"If he buried it, he'd have to dig it up, and Tyler was old. Burying his gold would have been too much work. But it could have been farther downstream." Travis frowned as he looked around him. "It's hard to remember."

He led the way downstream, and Katie followed. Trying to follow his reasoning, she supposed it was possible Tyler had kept his gold by the water where he'd panned it, but finding hidden gold after a hundred years? It didn't seem likely, but if there was a chance, the gold could save the ranch.

Yet time proved to be the enemy as minutes slipped relentlessly by and the wind picked up and the clouds above began to swirl. Katie shivered against the chill and felt the remnants of blind hope being blown away. She and Travis were chasing a dream. "We've got to go back, Travis."

He turned to look at her, frustration eating at his stomach. He was close. He could feel it. They couldn't give up. If they did, the ranch would be lost, and he would have failed again.

She saw his pain, recognized his desperation and knew its cause. He felt he'd failed Molly. He didn't want to fail her, too. "Tomorrow, Travis. Let's come back tomorrow."

Before he could argue, a streak of lightning cut the sky and thunder shook the earth. He swore at the clouds and the storm, at his own inability to do what he had to, but Katie's safety had to come first. The gold had remained buried for one hundred years. It could wait a day more. He motioned toward the path to the truck. "Come on! Let's get out of the rain!"

KATIE SET HER PLATE aside with a satisfied sigh. It felt good to have food in her stomach again. Not having eaten since breakfast hours earlier, she'd been starved. A glance at Travis, who sat across from her on the floor, told her he'd felt the same.

By the time they'd left the stream, their horses and saddles had been thoroughly drenched and the path back to the truck filled with mud. The expected summer shower had turned into a blistering thunderstorm complete with torrential rain and a pattering of hail. Poor visibility had made returning to the ranch out of the question. Instead she'd headed for the closest dry shelter—the Hunnicutt home.

Katie grinned as she watched Travis scrape his plate. Bare chested and barefoot, he sat with a blanket wrapped around his shoulders. His sodden shirt, boots and socks had been set out to dry, as had her own clothes. Fortunately, she'd been able to find more than just a blanket to wear. She'd shed all her clothes for a clean shirt someone had left behind. It was too big and stretched to her knees, but with the blanket she'd hitched around her waist like a skirt, she was warm and dry. And with a full stomach and the heat from the fire, she was beginning to feel human again.

She sighed again and closed her eyes as the fire continued to warm her thoroughly chilled body. It was doubtful she and Travis would get back to the ranch any time soon. The storm showed no sign of letting up, and it was late. Early evening already. But she didn't care. Away from the ranch, she could imagine it didn't exist, it or any of its problems. She opened her eyes again to meet the inquisitive gaze of the man who had made it easy to forget her worries.

"What are you thinking?" he asked.

She shrugged. "That the past is a wonderful place to be." She tilted her head to look around her. "Steve and Molly were happy here."

"They were."

"But what about you?" Her eyes came back to his. "You've told me all about them, about everyone else in Eagle River, but what about you? I want to know all about Sheriff Travis McCord."

He threw her a quick, self-conscious grin and set his plate aside. "I was born in 1865 in Abilene right about the time the war was ending and the cattle drives were starting. My mother was a schoolteacher, my father a bank teller."

"And he liked to gamble."

Travis smiled again. "Yes, he dragged my mother and me to one town after another. He spent his nights playing cards, and my mother spent them coaching me on my ABCs." Travis pushed his damp hair from his forehead and shrugged his shoulders beneath the blanket that remained draped around him. "I never got to make many friends. We moved too much, but every place we went I found out who the local lawman was and followed him around." His lips twisted with wry humor. "I don't know why. They just seemed big and important, and they didn't mind all my questions."

"So you became one?"

"Eventually." Travis frowned and shoved himself to his feet to restlessly walk to the window and stare out at the pounding rain. "First I tried gambling, mining and ranching."

"But you said you were a sheriff before coming to Eagle River."

"Yes, in Wyoming, but I'd been thinking about moving on to Montana where the gold and silver mines were when Ed Parrish came looking for help."

Katie frowned. "He was a storekeeper, wasn't he?"

"Yes, I told you about him. He was a good man, ran the general store, and he knew the hostility growing between the miners and ranchers couldn't continue or someone was going to get hurt. With the consent of the other shopkeepers, when he went to Wyoming on business, Ed stopped by the territorial marshal's office and asked for a reference."

"And you were there."

Travis nodded. "I was in the office and had been telling the marshal how quiet things had gotten. I guess he knew I was getting itchy feet, and he volunteered me when Ed Parrish asked if he knew anyone who could be hired as sheriff."

"That's when you met Steve and Molly." He nodded, and she watched his eyes caress the room around him.

"I helped them build this house."

"You said I looked like Molly."

Travis turned to her where she sat on the floor. With wet hair and wrapped in a man's shirt and a wool blanket, she looked small and fragile. His chest tightened. "You do, but your hair's different. Hers was auburn, but she had hazel eyes like you. And she was small like you." He smiled. "I thought she was the most beautiful woman I'd ever known."

Katie's eyes caught and held his. "Were you in love with her?"

He shook his head. "No, I just wanted to be."

"Good." She rose to walk to him. "Do you still blame yourself for her death?"

Travis frowned. "I want to believe I could have prevented it. Now I'm not so sure I could have."

"You couldn't."

The declaration was fierce, and he smiled and reached out to touch her cheek. She'd taken the guilt away. She was good for him. Could he be good for her?

She saw his eyes darken. "Travis, you said you came to the future for me, to help me with the ranch, and you've tried. Everybody has, but what if all we've done isn't enough? What if I lose it? Will I lose you, too?"

The tears that gathered in her eyes had him pulling her to him. "You're not going to lose the ranch. We're going to find Tyler's gold, and with it you can pay off all the debts, start again."

"But what about you?"

"I don't know."

He wouldn't meet her eyes, and she sensed his fear. "Will you stay with me?"

Travis struggled with black uncertainty. The future wasn't something he was sure he'd be allowed to see. "Katie—"

She stamped a foot. "You can't go, Travis McCord! You can't just come into my life and then ride off into the sunset!"

He frowned. "Why would I want to do that?"

Katie gestured futilely. "Never mind. It's a stupid thing heroes in the cowboy movies always do."

"Oh."

Her gaze locked with his. "I don't want you to go."

"I don't know if I can stay."

Katie's heart stopped beating. "You mean because you're supposed to be dead?" Her hand covered his. "I won't believe that!"

Travis pulled away. "You know it's true. I was killed—"

"But you didn't die! You're alive. You're here."

"But I don't know for how long." He shook his head. "I don't know how I got here. I don't know what it means. I've been given a second chance, but if I do what I'm supposed to, can I finish my life or will I just be allowed to rest easy?"

Katie moved to him. "You can't die!"

"I don't want to leave you."

"Then don't." She clutched his waist. His flesh was warm against her palms. "You don't have to go. You can stay with me. I know it's strange, but you've already learned so much!" Her eyes searched his. "Stay with me, Travis. I need you."

He folded her against his chest. She wanted him to stay. He closed his eyes and let the warmth of her words fill him while the warmth of her body brought him comfort. Yet he didn't know if he had a choice.

His skin was smooth against her hands and cheek. She couldn't imagine being without him. Not hearing his voice, seeing his face, being able to touch him. She turned her head and pressed her lips to his chest.

Travis gasped at the unexpected contact, and desire rocketed through him as she kissed him again.

She liked the taste of him, the feel of his flesh and the response of his muscles beneath her palms. Her hands caressed the smooth expanse of his back, but before she could further her explorations, his hands were suddenly in her hair pulling her head back and his mouth was on hers.

The blanket slipped from his shoulders as he pulled her more firmly into his grasp. It fell unnoticed to the floor as her arms wound around his neck and her fingers tangled in his hair. The heat of her skin was scorching through the thin cotton shirt she wore, and he traced the slender lines of her body as she strained against him.

Surrounded by his strength, she felt as if she was being absorbed. His lips teased and coaxed while his hands stimulated. She clutched at his shoulders to meet his mouth again.

Pulling her upward as she stretched on tiptoe, he caught and held her to him, unmindful that the blanket hitched around her waist had loosened and slowly slid to the floor to join his. He groaned silently as her body rubbed against and tormented his. Her breasts pressed into his chest. Her fingers stroked and searched.

Arching backward she clung fiercely to him, bare legs rubbing against the damp roughness of his jeans. The irritating scrape of the material seemed to heighten the pleasure his touch wrought on the other planes of her body, and she trembled as his head dropped and he ravaged her throat. But suddenly his hands grabbed her waist, and she gasped as he lifted her over his head.

Holding her above him, he stared into her eyes. Gold flames burned in pools of brown. Slowly he lowered her to him. Their lips met, and he felt both her legs wrap around one of his. A shudder shook him.

Liquid fire. She was melting against him again, and
the heat of her embrace threatened to consume him.

Held slightly above and draped down one side of his
body, she wound her arms around his neck to lend
support as her legs used the strength of his as solid
ground. His lips covered hers in gentle persuasion.
Their tongues touched, and she gasped again as the
rough width of his palm found her bare thigh and
moved up to cup her buttocks. "Travis!"

The word was a plea, and abruptly his grip shifted.
He swung her down, only to catch her against his chest
with one arm under her knees and the other beneath
her shoulders. He turned and strode across the floor,
away from the fire and into one of the side rooms. A
bunk bed waited, and he set her down gently.

She reached up to guide him to her, savoring the
strength of his shoulders as one of his hands again
found a bare thigh to follow. She squirmed beneath
him at the slow caress over sensitive skin that led his
fingers to tangle in the tails of her shirt.

Buttons gave and material slipped over smooth flesh
as, with impatient motions, he pushed the shirt she
wore open to reveal the skin beneath. His eyes devoured her exposed flesh before he lowered his head to
plunder new ground.

She writhed in trembling ecstasy as his lips, teeth
and tongue tasted and teased, and she buried her
hands in the thickness of his hair as his mouth explored each of her breasts with aching thoroughness.
She was on fire.

He slipped his hands around her to lift her into a
sitting position. Quickly the shirt was discarded to
leave her naked beside him, but before her hands could

carry him to her once more, he rolled away to swiftly strip off his jeans.

She welcomed him back into her embrace with a quiet sigh. His strength surrounded her. His legs tangled with hers. The soft hair covering his chest seemed rough against her breasts, but his touch was gentle.

Entwined together, they rolled as one across the narrow confines of the bed. Hands and lips explored as they each sought to learn, until the need to consume became stronger than the desire to merely touch. Limbs moved and flesh gave as she accepted what he wanted to give.

Driven to please as well as to be pleased, he filled her with a pulsing rhythm. It carried them both upward on a roaring tide that crested on a thundering wave. Release came with a cry, crashing over them in a flood of wondrous sensation, that left them bathed in love's sweet aftermath.

Katie lay cradled against Travis. His arms were around her. She felt safe and secure and immensely satisfied as she listened to the mad pounding of his heart beneath her ear. Never had she experienced such a sense of belonging, of completeness. She closed her eyes and savored the warmth and protection he offered.

Slowly his breathing returned to normal. He felt overwhelmed. No woman had ever responded to him the way Katie had, giving herself without reservation and in complete abandon. He had felt more than the duty to return every pleasure he'd received. He wanted her to know how much she meant to him. "Katie."

But as his arms tightened and his lips touched her brow, she put up a hand to stop any words. She didn't want anything to disturb the peace she'd found. No doubts, no fears. Not the future or the past. "Just hold me."

And he did, until passion started to burn once more, and they rode the tide again and again before the night passed and they found sleep in each other's arms.

Chapter Thirteen

Katie stood watching Travis check the horses. They were back at Tyler's shack. The storm had passed, the skies were clear, but the night's passing had done its damage. The wind had toppled the old barn, and it had heightened her fear, her fear of losing him. "Travis, we don't have to go."

He dropped a stirrup after tightening the cinch and looked at her from across the horse's back. "You're wrong. I have this to do, Katie, and I'm going to do it. I'm not going to fail you like I failed Molly."

Katie rushed around the horse to grab his arm. "You didn't fail Molly, and you haven't failed me. If finding the gold means losing you, I'd rather not have it!"

He caught her arms. "Listen to me, Katie. I don't know what the future is, but I know what it should be. You should keep the ranch. It's yours. Steve and Molly built it for you—for all their children and their children's children. It's what should be, and I'm not going to be the cause of you losing it."

Fighting tears, she watched him turn away. "I won't help you!"

"Then I'll do it myself." Travis threw himself into the saddle and looked down at her. "No matter what happens to me, Katie, I have to know you'll be safe—whether I can stay or not."

Tears blurred her vision. She couldn't stop him. "Then I'm coming with you."

At the stream Travis sat staring at the land around him. One hundred years had wrought enough changes, but the storm had made more. Tree limbs had been torn off and tossed about, the wind and pounding rain had caused part of the wall leading up from the stream to cave in. His jaw tightened as he surveyed the damage. Time and nature were working against him, but he wasn't going to fail.

In silence Katie followed him as he rode away from the stream and onto the land beyond. When he stopped his horse and turned around she met his gaze with anxious eyes.

"I'm going to try going back to the stream exactly the way I did that day when I found Tyler. The land's changed, but the stream's still where it was. That means his gold is still there, too."

Not wanting to doubt him, Katie remained silent and meekly trailed after him, trying to decide if she wanted him to succeed or not. He wouldn't quit until he did, but that was small comfort since his success might mean she'd lose him forever.

Approaching the stream from another angle, the one he remembered, Travis tried to drag all the details of the past from his mind. Where had he been exactly, and where had Tyler been coming from? He stopped, recognizing a cut in the trail leading from the shack to the stream. "Tyler was coming from that direction."

Slowly, meticulously, they searched. Walking their horses carefully along the streambed, they looked for something, anything, to tell them Tyler had once been there. But one pass revealed nothing, and the return trip was no more encouraging.

Travis swore under his breath, frustration eating at his insides. He was close. He knew it. They couldn't give up. If they did, the ranch would be lost, and that couldn't happen. If he had to leave, he wasn't going to leave Katie destitute. "Damn it, Tyler! Where'd you put it!"

"Travis."

He ignored her outstretched hand and swung his horse back up the stream again. "Maybe we have to go farther."

Once more they followed the stream's current, looking for anything that would point to what had been, but all they saw was mud and rock.

Yanking his horse to a halt, Travis swung to the ground. "All right, Tyler. You're not going to make this easy and knowing how you loved that gold, I shouldn't expect you to."

Katie watched Travis start off on foot, slipping through mud as he started the search from the point where he'd last seen the old miner. Biting her lip, she slid from the saddle to follow.

Mud sucked at their feet, and branches tore at their legs and arms as they pushed their way along what could have been a path. But it proved a dead end. They were forced back, but Travis wasn't about to give up. Returning to the streambed, he found another trail and then another, and Katie followed him down each one as the sun climbed into the sky and the land began to dry. He needed to do what he thought he must.

She wanted to help him because he felt success was so important, but she dreaded each step might be the last they would take together.

Struggling up yet one more slippery incline, Travis reached down to give Katie a hand up. Desperation was near. Time was working against him. She stumbled to his side, and he held her close while they stood together gulping air and searching the wall that stretched up before them. Both he and she were dirty. Mud smeared their clothes, their hands, their faces.

"Travis, so much has changed. Are you sure this is where you last saw Tyler?"

"Yes. He was coming from this direction and was going down toward the stream." Travis looked around him. "It looked different then. The wall was here, but there was more ground leading up to it."

"A path?"

He nodded. "I think so." His eyes searched the rocks and hardy brush clinging to the wall. "I can't believe he'd have hidden the gold much farther away than this. It's got to be close!"

Her fingers intertwined with his. "With as much damage as this last storm did, maybe whatever cave or hole Tyler used has been buried."

"No, I won't believe that. Tyler was coming down. That meant the gold was up. It shouldn't have been buried or washed away." Travis fought to keep his footing as he tried to follow the ground upward. "If I just knew what I was looking for!"

Katie moved after him, putting a hand out to the wall to steady herself, but it wasn't enough when her foot slipped. She cried out as the mud gave way, and grabbed wildly for support. Her fingers hit some stiff brush rooted firmly into the dirt, and she hung on.

The branches snapped but held under her weight, and Travis lunged to grab her.

He caught her arm, and relying on the heavy brush for continued support, he leaned out to drag her up.

Floundering for a foothold, she fought for balance until, abruptly, he pulled, and together they fell back against the wall. But the dirt wasn't solid as it appeared. With a startled cry Katie clung to Travis as they tumbled into the brush and the gouge in the earth that lay behind it.

Travis swore as he fought his way free from the clinging bite of the branches, but when he had finally helped to free Katie, his angry glare at the broken bush turned into a disbelieving stare. With a gleeful whoop he dived back into the bush.

Katie jumped back in alarm as he began tearing wildly at the branches, ripping it out by the roots. She was sure he'd gone mad. Dirt and leaves flew around her, but then, suddenly, she saw it, too.

The gouge they'd fallen into hadn't merely been a hole in the wall. Instead the dark gash appeared to be an opening of some kind. Taller than it was wide, it almost looked like a tunnel into the earth.

"Travis!"

"This must be the hiding place," he told her. "We're close now." But he'd almost missed it. The entrance had been concealed well, and time had encouraged the bushes and undergrowth around it to further camouflage the mouth to a cave.

Katie watched in openmouthed amazement as he went back to fighting with the bush. Then she began working with him, and together they pulled and yanked until enough of the growth had been cleared away to let them inside.

Travis held her back with a gesture when she moved to step in before him. "Better let me go first, just in case. We might be sharing this with some unfriendly visitors." He pulled the Colt from its holster and squeezed through the gap in the ridge wall.

Katie shivered as he disappeared, fear and anticipation mixing in a muddled blend of excitement. She bit her lip and studied the black slit in the earth. Was it really a cave, or did they only hope it was? A sudden flicker of light from inside killed any doubts. "Travis?"

"Come on in!"

She followed his voice, worming her way past branches and through the dirt walls toward the light. The ceiling was low, but a few feet in it finally lifted. She stumbled into a little cave where Travis stood holding a lamp.

"Tyler was good enough to leave us a lantern," he told her with a grin.

She grinned back and looked at the dented kerosene lamp in his hand. It was old and bent, but it still worked.

Travis held up the lantern so it illuminated the shadowy corners. They were surrounded by rock walls, but another tunnel of sorts stood off to the left. "This looks to be the first cavern." He stepped toward the opening, only to have Katie grab his arm.

"Travis!" The excitement had blinded her, made her forget.

He smiled at the fear in her eyes. "It'll be all right."

Reluctantly she let him go. Could she really hope for gold and Travis, too? Could she have both? She'd settle for one. She wanted him.

He gestured at the dusty ground. "It doesn't look like anyone or anything has been through here in a long time, but you'd best stay behind me."

With his Colt in one hand and the lamp in the other, Travis cautiously entered the tunnel, and Katie followed. The ceiling dropped again, and the walls closed in. She thought they'd reached the end when Travis swore.

"Damn Tyler, anyway. He was almost as small as you are."

Katie bit her lip as Travis moved forward and disappeared around a corner. The walls were dark and damp and close. She shivered and followed with her head down to avoid the cavern's roof and ended up running straight into Travis as she exited the tunnel. He was standing stiff and still before her. Frowning, she straightened to her full height and looked around him to find what he was staring at. The breath immediately caught in her throat.

Without a word he moved forward to set the kerosene lamp down next to a pile of small leather sacks. He knelt and slid his Colt back into its holster as she fell to her knees beside him. "I think we're about to find out if Tyler was lying or not."

She watched as Travis picked up one of the sacks to pull at the leather thong holding it closed. He tipped the contents into his palm, and she gasped when a scattering of glittering dust and small nuggets rolled into his hand. "Is it . . . ?"

He held it up to the lantern light and pushed his finger through it. "Real?" He sent her a somersaulting grin. "Tyler wasn't any fool. This is pure American gold."

With a cry of joy she threw her arms around Travis's neck but drew back just enough to stare down at his hand. Hope was returning. They'd found the gold. But, more, Travis was still with her. He hadn't disappeared. The past hadn't taken him from her. Nevertheless, she kept a firm grip on his arm. "How much do you think there is?" Her voice was barely above a whisper.

"At least enough to build a new barn."

She laughed and hugged him again. "I can't believe it!"

"Believe it," he told her, putting the gold back in its bag. "And it's all yours."

She sat back to look at him. "Ours."

Hope ignited in him, too. He wasn't dead yet. He grinned and pulled her into his lap to cover her mouth with his. "Yours," he repeated firmly when he lifted his lips from hers. Tears shone in her eyes as she raised a hand to touch his face, but the tears abruptly erupted into laughter as the realization of what the gold meant began to sink in.

"I can't wait to tell the bank!"

Travis's laughter mixed with hers, the sound echoing off the walls of the small cavern that had hidden one man's riches for more than a hundred years. "I think they'll be very happy when you make your next deposit."

She reached up to pull his head down to hers. She lay against his chest, clinging to the solid strength of him. He was real. The gold was real. "Oh, Travis, what would I have done without you?"

"I'm here."

His voice was strong and sure, but her smile trembled. "You can stay now."

The statement was hesitant, almost a question, a plea, but he wanted to believe the present would last. He lifted one hand to point to the gold. "We'd better get this out of here before we run out of kerosene."

Katie shivered and slipped off his lap. Being trapped in a cave without light, even with Travis, wasn't something she was eager to experience. "What should we do?"

"I'll squeeze back through to the other side, and you can hand me the bags. Once we have them all in the other cavern, we can go back to the horses to get the saddlebags and load up." He grinned. "Then we can go and see your banker."

She laughed. "I'm ready!"

It was slow work for the two of them in the cramped confines of the tunnel, and it was hours before they were able to get all of the gold, packaged away in countless small sacks, into the outer cavern.

"We'll have to make more than one trip to the truck," Travis told her with a shake of his head. "Tyler's left you more gold than even I imagined."

Kneeling beside Travis in the small cave, she looked up into his dirt-streaked face. "I still can't believe this is happening. Tyler must have mined for years to have accumulated this much gold."

"His whole life."

"And he never spent it." She shook her head. "It's sad. Money might not buy happiness, but it could have made him a lot more comfortable."

"Don't feel sorry for him, Katie. Tyler was happy in his own way. He found his dream."

"Gold." A mischievous grin curved her lips. "I suppose this means I'll have to give you a raise."

Travis grinned and stood, being careful to watch his head. "Me and everyone else."

She laughed and bent to pick up one set of the very heavy saddlebags.

TRAVIS BROUGHT the truck to a bumpy halt outside the garage that housed the ranch equipment.

"You only killed the engine three times," Katie told him as she relaxed her grip on the dashboard. "I think you're getting better."

He threw her a grin. "Maybe we ought to ask the horses."

"How can we? I think we left them on the road at the last turn!"

"You guys finally made it back!"

Travis looked up to find Mike at the window. "Miss us?"

"Thought you'd found your gold and run off into the hills," Mike answered as Travis swung the truck door open and stepped out.

"No. We came back to give you your share."

Mike rolled his eyes and looked over at Katie, who had climbed out the passenger side. As muddy as they both were, he could almost believe they had been digging for gold. "Got caught by the storm?"

"We were closer to the Hunnicutt homestead than here so when it started hailing, we took cover there," she answered, avoiding Mike's eyes as she walked around the hood to join him and Travis on the driver's side. She wondered how much her love of Travis showed.

"That's what I told everyone." Mike nodded with satisfaction. "That storm was a real humdinger."

She met him at the end of the trailer, and her expression was suddenly worried. "Was it bad here?"

"Lots of lightning and thunder and wind, but no damage. We got the horses out of it by moving the equipment out of the garage."

Katie nodded in relief but felt guilt at having neglected her duties toward the ranch. Her foreman was gone. She should have been there to give orders and protect what was hers.

"Maybe Ms. Shannon should make you foreman, Mike," Travis said, recognizing and soothing her worries at the same time. "Seeing as you're so good at taking charge."

Mike flushed with pleasure. "Wasn't nothing. Besides, it wasn't just me that did it. Gus and the others helped."

Katie's eyes strayed to the black ruins of the barn. "We'll have to build the stock a bigger and better barn. I'll call someone tomorrow to see how fast we can get it done."

Mike grinned. "Great thing, insurance."

Katie met Travis's eyes. He knew she'd let that policy lapse as well as the one on the cattle, but it didn't matter anymore. The depression she'd been in when the barn had burned was gone, lifted by the discovery of gold that could get most, if not all, of the wrongs of the past year put right. "Isn't it?"

Mike jerked his thumb over his shoulder toward the house. "You've got company, by the way."

She looked past him to the big silver and little black sports cars. "Simon and Ken."

"Been waiting since this morning."

And it was almost dusk. Her eyes returned to Travis.

"I'll help you get the bags up to the house," he reassured her. The night before he'd told her that finding the gold, helping her save the ranch, was what he'd come to do, but was it enough? Was that why he hadn't gone back to the past after finding Tyler's cache? Katie might not be safe yet. Those who had tried to bring about her downfall were still waiting somewhere. Would whoever it was stop now that she had money to fight with? Or would that someone still want the ranch and try to see to it that she met with an accident, too?

Mike frowned as Travis leaned into the truck and the front seat to retrieve two pairs of saddlebags. "You didn't really find gold," he said in disbelief. The bags looked awfully heavy.

Travis just grinned and held out an arm to Katie. "Be back in a minute to help you with the horses. Then you can help me unload the rest."

"The rest . . ." They left Mike stammering.

She fell into step beside Travis, liking the feel of his fingers as they settled on her waist. "No one's ever going to believe we did find gold."

"Not until they see it," he admitted.

She led the way up the steps, excitement building at the thought of actually spreading the news, but she stopped suddenly when she reached the door. The house was where she belonged. But not without Travis. Could she convince a man from the 1800s to throw convention aside and move in with her? "Travis—"

"The bunkhouse just isn't going to be the same," he told her quietly and lifted a gentle hand to brush her cheek. Her clothes were wrinkled from the soaking by the storm and the drying in front of the fire, and mud soiled her jeans and blouse, but he didn't notice. He saw only the want in her eyes. "The bed might be the same size, but it'll seem awful empty."

She caught his hand, but before she could speak, the door abruptly opened behind her.

"I thought I heard a truck pull in," Simon said, and opened his arms to reach for Katie. "Thank God you're all right!"

"You shouldn't have worried," she told him, returning his embrace before letting him lead her through the door and toward the study. A silent glance over her shoulder beckoned Travis to follow.

"We were both worried!"

Katie turned at the exclamation to find Ken standing by the fireplace inside the study. "I'm sorry. As you can see, there was no need. I'm fine."

"It would have been nice if you'd let us know," he said, following her with angry eyes as she advanced into the room toward the desk. "First, on Friday night, we run into Mark Harrison who tells us he's quit. The next morning we hear about the barn burning down—not from you but from someone else—and then you disappear! No one knew where you went!"

Katie stopped behind the desk to face him. "Mike knew where I'd gone."

Ken laughed. "Out looking for gold! Really, Katie, you should have thought of someone besides yourself. Simon's been frantic."

She looked at her stepfather. "If you were worried, Simon, I really am sorry. So much had happened. I just didn't think—"

"Were you thinking when you let Mark Harrison walk out?" Ken asked.

Katie glared at him. "He was out of line, and I didn't ask him to leave. He did it himself."

"Because you wouldn't back him up when it came to Travis McCord," Ken objected. "You can't expect a foreman to stay on if he doesn't get your support."

"He was wrong, and I'm glad he's gone," Katie returned sharply, her temper igniting. "None of the men liked him, and he didn't help me very much."

"Maybe you wouldn't let him."

"Maybe he didn't try." All eyes in the room turned to Travis where he leaned against the door with the saddlebags over his shoulder. He centered his attention on a wide-eyed Ken Baxter.

"He came highly recommended," Ken objected, straightening to his full height as he met the cold blue of Travis's stare from across the room.

"You were the one who found him for Katie?" Travis asked, and looked at Simon. "I assumed it was you."

Simon shrugged. "I know nothing of ranching, and with all of Ken's connections, he asked around. Mark Harrison's name came up, and Ken suggested him."

Travis nodded and looked back to see Ken swing toward Katie.

"I should have known you'd be out with him when you disappeared." Ken pointed to Travis. "I suppose you're considering making him your new foreman?"

"Maybe," Katie agreed with a tilt to her chin.

"You can't be serious! If you can believe him, which I don't, the man's only credentials are as former sheriff of a ghost town!"

"I wouldn't say *only*."

The tone of her voice had all three men looking at her, but only Travis was grinning.

Flushing but not backing down under their scrutiny, she quickly continued as a heavy silence filled the room. "He's very good with horses."

Ken swore under his breath. Simon silently looked from her to Travis, who moved forward and put the saddlebags on the desk.

Travis met Katie's gaze. "I'd better go help Mike with the horses." But as he turned to go, she stopped him.

"Why don't you stay until I show them what we found?" She didn't want him to leave, and it was his discovery as well as hers. She wanted to share it with him. He stopped and nodded silently, and she smiled before looking at the two other men in the room. "Both of you know there's been a lot of problems with the ranch and that I had to get a loan from the bank. What you don't know is that I let the insurance go on the cattle, so when the rustlers came, I couldn't get any reimbursement. I also let the property insurance lapse, which means I won't get any help with the barn."

"Katie," Simon murmured in sympathetic understanding.

"No, let me finish, Simon," she insisted, and sent him a brilliant smile. "I know you want to help. You've been trying to help ever since Mom died, but now I'm in a position to help you."

Moving to the far wall to stand, Travis watched Simon exchange a baffled look with Ken.

Katie pulled at the straps of one of the saddlebags. "You see, when Travis took me out yesterday looking for gold, I thought it was just something he was doing because he was trying to make me feel better, but I was wrong."

Both men's glances came back to her.

"The two of you know Travis worked at Eagle River." As Ken crossed his arms over his chest, she added, "Ken, your investigator couldn't find any record of the state or county hiring Travis because Travis was working there on his own. He shares a love of the past like I do and was doing...research." A glance at Travis found him grinning. She grinned, too, and hurried on. "By putting a few clues together about Tyler Fenton and his murder, Travis came up with this." She pulled out one of the pouches and poured some of the contents into her hand. "Gold."

Nobody moved. Nobody breathed until Simon suddenly collapsed into a chair. "Gold." His face was white and Katie started to move to him in alarm, but he waved her back. "No, I'm all right. Just stunned. I—I can't believe it."

She grinned. "Neither can I, but isn't it wonderful?"

Slowly Ken came forward and stopped before the desk to stare at the dust in her hand. "Are you sure it's real?"

"It's real," Travis answered for her, earning a narrowed glare from Ken.

"The bags are full of this?" Ken asked.

"And there's more in the truck," Katie told him. "Mike's watching it."

Ken looked again at Travis. "I suppose you're going to help yourself to at least half?"

Travis stiffened, and Katie protested. "That's unfair, Ken! If it hadn't been for Travis, I wouldn't have found this. He didn't have to tell me. He could have taken it all for himself, and I'd never have known about it."

Ken shoved his hands into his pockets and stared hard at her. "So with this you have everything you need or want."

"I have a new barn and a new chance."

"And a new foreman." The muscles in Ken's jaw jumped. "Obviously I'm not needed anymore." He turned to look at Simon. "I'll see you in town, Simon." And without another word he strode from the room.

Katie watched him go with a puzzled frown. "I thought everyone would be happy with the news."

Simon pushed himself from the chair. The color was back in his face. "We are, honey, it's just—" he gestured expressively "—we're overwhelmed." He stopped by the desk to take one of the pouches from the saddlebags. "You're certainly going to make the bank's day tomorrow."

She laughed and looked at Travis, who remained standing quietly at the far side of the room. "Will you ride shotgun with me tomorrow, Sheriff?"

A quick smile came to his lips. "Yes, ma'am. I'll even stand guard tonight." But his thoughts were sober as he watched her. Ken Baxter's reaction had been that of a bitter man. How much had he been relying on Katie's marrying him and selling the ranch? And what of Simon? It wasn't a normal reaction to turn white at the sight of gold. Slowly he, too, approached the desk, but he was worried. He feared Katie's fight wasn't over yet.

Chapter Fourteen

Two weeks later Travis stood in the ranch yard watching the pickup carrying Mike and Gus grow smaller as it followed the road out of the yard toward town. He grinned as it disappeared around the bend. It was high noon on Saturday, and the place was deserted. He and Katie were going to be alone at last.

Smothering the urge to shout, Travis headed for the house with long-legged strides. The past days had been busy. A new barn was up, the cattle had gone to market and, despite waiting for some unknown evil to rear its head, nothing had happened. No more accidents. No more crises. He was beginning to doubt a conspiracy to take the ranch from Katie had ever existed.

He'd been leery after Simon's and Ken's reactions to the gold find, but neither man had anything to gain by Katie's selling the ranch. And while Mark Harrison could have been responsible for putting the rustlers on the cattle and for setting the fire, he hadn't been seen or heard of since he'd quit.

Leaping the steps, Travis aimed for the porch. The deaths of Pauline Shannon Griffith and Bill Henry could have been nothing more than tragic fatalities motivated by nothing more than fate. The rustlers could have been a mere coincidence. Somehow he doubted it, but anyone after the ranch had apparently given up once the gold had been deposited in the bank, and that was fine with him. He and Katie had better use for their time than worrying—now that it looked as if he was staying in the future for good.

Travis hit the top stair and nearly ran straight into Helen Henry as she came out the front door. They both jumped back in surprise.

"Travis McCord, you just took another year off my life!"

He grinned unrepentantly. "Didn't expect to see you here."

She looked him up and down with a critical eye that didn't find much wrong with the man before her. "Don't expect you did, but here I am and here Katie isn't."

Disappointment hit him hard.

"Yes, she was expecting you, and she looked about as happy as you do right now when Simon showed up and asked her to go out gallivanting with him." Helen gestured over her shoulder to the door. "She and I were going over the grocery list when he came. Said he'd like to see the place where she found the gold."

"Simon?"

"Yes, I know. Hard to figure, but gold does strange things to people." Helen shook her head. "Though I can't imagine him getting dirty going into the cave. Katie said to tell you that she'd be back as quick as she could."

Helen moved away, and Travis stood alone on the porch and sighed. So much for making plans, but as he took his first step toward the bunkhouse, he came to a halt. Simon wanted to see where the gold had

been hidden. Helen was right. It was hard to imagine
Simon squeezing his way into a cave. He was always
meticulous about his appearance. He never had a hair
or a button out of place. Travis looked for Simon's
car, but it wasn't in sight. Surely Katie wouldn't have
taken Simon's elegant silver machine out to Tyler's
place. They'd have no horses then, and Simon would
have to walk to the cave.

Suddenly Travis remembered Simon at the dinner
table after the gold had been brought home. He'd been
teasing Katie about being rich.

"You don't need the ranch now, Katie. You can go
anywhere and live wherever you want. Why not sell it
and go find a palace to live in?"

"What would I do in a palace?" Katie had laughed.

"Be the queen you deserve to be. No more hard
work. You can have a stable full of horses to ride every
day. No more stalls to muck out or cattle to herd." He
had looked at her across the table. "Seriously, Katie,
why not sell and move on?"

"I couldn't sell the ranch, Simon. It's home, and I'd
miss running it—and you'd miss seeing me."

Katie had laughed then at the concern in Simon's
eyes, but had it been concern? Travis tried to quell the
sense of panic that abruptly knotted his stomach.
Since he'd met Simon, he'd been touched by the worry
the man always directed at Katie, but had it been
worry for Katie or for himself? Could Simon possibly
be the one trying to force Katie out of her own home?

Travis didn't want to believe it. He didn't understand it. How could Simon gain anything from Katie
losing the ranch? But how didn't matter.

Leaping from the porch, Travis raced after Helen, who was halfway across the yard. He skidded to a halt and grabbed her arm. "How long ago did they leave?"

"No more than half an hour, why?" But Travis didn't answer. He ran for the bunkhouse, and she called after him, "You can probably catch them! Simon doesn't like to drive very fast!"

Travis reached his cube and his dresser and yanked open the bottom drawer. Clothes scattered across the floor as he pulled the Colt free before swinging immediately back toward the door and the Jeep Katie always left parked with the keys in it. He had a chance. If he could get the Jeep started and keep it running, he could catch them. He could circle in behind Tyler's place and meet them there by going the back way.

He threw himself into the Jeep but abruptly stopped to stare at the pedals on the floor. The only thing he had to do was stay calm and remember everything Katie had taught him about driving. There could be no killing the engine this time. If he did, it could mean Katie's life. He reached for the keys.

KATIE SAT in the passenger seat, swaying from side to side as Simon drove her over the rolling land toward Tyler Fenton's shack. She smothered a smile as the car dipped precariously over another embankment. Why Simon had insisted on driving, she didn't know. His car was a prize toy that was presently getting the springs rocked out of it, but he'd been determined to be the chauffeur.

Glancing at him as he concentrated on driving over the uneven ground leading toward their destination, Katie silently shook her head. She was glad Simon had taken an interest in the past. She just wished he hadn't decided to choose the weekend to do it. Chewing at her lip, she thought of Travis and the afternoon they'd planned to share. They had talked of going on a picnic. At least, he had. She hadn't intended to let him get out the door once he'd gotten in. After all, she never had given him a tour of the house.

She swallowed a sigh. She'd tried to convince Simon to wait so that Travis could come with them, but Simon had wanted to do it alone with her.

"We're almost there, aren't we?" Simon asked, interrupting her thoughts.

"Almost," Katie agreed, sending him a smile. She'd taken him the least bumpy route she could think of, but the rangeland of Montana wasn't meant to be a roadway for anything other than four-wheel-drive vehicles, horses and cattle.

"It must have been exciting to find the gold," he told her.

"It was. Until we got inside. It was dark and close, and Travis and I weren't even sure it was there."

"But it was, and now you're rich."

She reached over to squeeze his arm. "So are you." She leaned back in her seat. "I remember how you used to talk to Mom about expanding. Now you can. I'll give you a loan, no questions asked."

"I never thought otherwise, Katie, but I do wish you'd reconsider selling the ranch."

"But why?"

"It's a big responsibility. It always has been. If you sell it, you could be free. With the gold, you could travel. See the world. No more work. Only play."

"Simon, that's idealistic. You can't run from responsibility. Everybody has to carry their fair share. Besides, everyone needs a home, and mine is at the ranch. The Double S. Though I am thinking about changing it back to the Bar H." She turned to look at him, hoping to change the subject. Ever since her mother had died, Simon had tried to convince her to sell, and every conversation they had seemed to lead to discussing the possibility. "What do you think?"

"I think you should reconsider."

Katie rolled her eyes and was grateful to see the shack dead ahead. "We're here, Simon." He stopped the car in front of it. "And I won't reconsider."

Simon climbed slowly from the car as she got out and moved to stand by the hood. He walked with her the few remaining feet to Tyler Fenton's door. "Would you reconsider if I told you that I needed you to? That it might mean your life?"

She turned puzzled eyes on him. "Simon, what are you talking about?"

He put his hands in his pockets to pace slowly away, only to return again, an elegant man in elegant clothes, sadly out of place beside the ramshackle dwelling an old hermit had once called home. "There's something about me that you don't know, Katie. I like to gamble."

She shrugged. "It's legal, Simon. A lot of people do it."

"Not like I do."

Realization suddenly dawned when he wouldn't look her in the eye. "Simon, are you in trouble? In debt?"

"Oh, yes."

She bit her lip as his gaze slowly lifted to hers. The admission had cost him. Simon wasn't good at confession. "If you need money—"

"I need more than that. I need you to sell the ranch." He shook his head and held up his hand before she could speak again. "About a year before your mother died, I went to Las Vegas on a business trip."

"I remember."

"But it wasn't really business. At least, not for legitimate business. It was to see if I could find a way out of debt. I thought if I could get lucky, I could wipe the slate clean, but I only made it worse."

"You gambled what money you had away?"

"Yes, and I couldn't keep going without some cash coming in. I had to get a loan."

"You and Mom argued about money."

His lips curved into a sad smile. "More than once. She didn't like the way I spent it, and eventually she found out I did more than spend. I bet."

Katie felt her heart sink. "She gave you money?"

"No. She said it was my problem, but I ended up making it hers."

"I don't understand."

He sighed. "I got a loan, but not from your mother or a bank. And, when I had trouble making payments, the people who gave me the money made it clear they wanted it back. They gave me a time limit to pay up or promised to make an example of me." He gave her a wry smile. "They don't just do that in the movies, you know. When you deal with the kind of people I owe, death is a very real threat."

"But what happened? How can my selling the ranch help you?"

"I promised the ranch as collateral."

"You what?"

"Yes, and they want it."

Katie's mouth dropped open in surprise. "But with the gold, I can pay them off."

"Not enough. It's the principle of the thing. I promised them something, and I have to deliver. They can't have people backing out of their promises. It's bad for business."

"I don't believe this."

"Your mother didn't either. She told me that I should just go to the police."

"Oh, Simon." Katie started to reach for him, but he waved her back.

"She was a good woman, your mother. And she was smart. Even without my telling her, I think she knew what I was up to, and it hurt her." He sighed. "I never meant to do that, but I'm not strong like she was. Can you understand that, Katie?"

She swallowed the lump in her throat. "Mom still loved you."

He shook his head. "Not at the end. It was over for us. She didn't trust me anymore. If she hadn't died..." He shrugged expressively before turning earnest eyes on her. "You're my last chance, Katie. You can give them what they want."

She shook her head. "Simon, I have the gold now. I can't give up the ranch."

"Katie, you don't understand the people I'm dealing with!"

The shout had Katie staggering back from him. She'd never heard Simon yell before.

"After your mother died I tried to convince you to sell in every way I knew how. I found Ken for you. He loves you, you know, and he would have taken you away. He's rich enough. You would have lived in style." Simon shook his head. "When I talked to him

about the ranch and what a burden it was, he even
agreed to help me convince you to sell it, and he got
me Mark Harrison."

Katie shook her head. "I don't understand."

"Mark was no find. He'd been a foreman before. A
bad one. He'd been fired, but he was perfect for us.
We gave him a second chance, knowing he'd run the
ranch into the ground, but you wouldn't listen to him.
When he wanted to sell cattle, you wouldn't do it."

"He wanted to strip the range!"

"But without cattle, you'd have to sell."

Katie stared at Simon in disbelief. This was a man
she'd thought she knew.

"Mark called in to me all the time. He told me
where the cattle were, and to keep the men from Vegas off my back, I asked them to send rustlers in to use
the steers as interest on the loan."

"You sent the rustlers!" Fury replaced disbelief.
"You tried to ruin me!"

"I was desperate, Katie! I still am. You've got to
help me!"

Katie's fists clenched. "I'll help you, all right. I'll
help you pay them back the loan out of the gold I
found, but they can't have the ranch, Simon. I won't
give it to them, and I won't give anything else to you
when this is done."

"You're wasting your breath, Simon, and your time
is up."

Katie spun to watch a man appear from around the
corner of the shack. Tall and elegantly dressed in a
perfectly tailored suit, he casually adjusted the cuff of
his shirt as he stopped a short distance from her.
"Who are you? What are you doing here?"

"Helping Simon out of the mess he got himself into."

"No," Simon interrupted, stepping forward. "Leave her alone. I can convince her."

"I don't think so."

Katie looked from one man to the other. Recognition came hard. Simon had led her into a trap. "You're working for the people Simon owes."

"Yes, and you've cost us a good deal of time and effort," the man told her, his gray eyes ice cold as he looked down at her. "We thought you'd give up once you found the debts your mother left, but when you hung on, we decided to speed things up."

Katie frowned. "How do you know about the debts?"

"Ask Simon."

Simon's face fell, and he avoided her eyes as she stared at him. "It's my fault the last checks didn't go out. Your mother always gave me the mail, remember? I hung on to all the checks, hoping somehow I could change her mind, but before she could even realize what was happening, she fell from her horse. To cover up, I used her key before you thought to take it and got rid of all the old drafts and statements. I cleaned out the desk."

"But it wasn't enough to stop you," the man said. "And when my boss got impatient, we had to find a way to hurry things along. You're the reason Bill Henry died."

Katie gasped. "You killed him?"

"He was in the way."

Numb with shock, she could only stare at him and then at Simon. It hadn't been the ranch turning against her with all its problems. It had been two men. One of whom she'd always trusted.

"But then this McCord showed up." The man's mouth thinned. "We had the rustlers all set up to go. We figured to make a nice profit off your beef, but after we got the first shipment, McCord got in the way. Without his interference, the loss of beef would have forced you to sell."

Katie glared at him. "Too bad for you."

He reached out to catch her chin with his finger. "You've made it an interesting game."

She slapped his hand away and turned to Simon, anger and hatred growing. "How could you?"

"I would have taken care of you," he objected lamely.

"Until when? Until you gambled again?" She whirled to face the stranger, unconsciously crossing her arms in front of her to ward off the black menace of his presence. "You can go back to your boss and tell him to stuff it. I'll never sell the ranch. Never!"

He clicked his tongue. "You'd better reconsider. You either sign on the dotted line and willingly walk away from the ranch—and the gold you just found on it that rightly belongs to us—or what happened to your mother is going to happen to you. You're going to meet with an accident."

Katie's breath caught in her throat, and her arms dropped to her sides. "My mother! You killed my mother?"

The man smiled, but Simon unexpectedly wailed.

"No! That's not true! You never told me that! That wasn't part of the deal, Thacker!"

Simon received a disparaging glance. "The deal was for you to get us the ranch. You weren't doing the job, so we decided to help."

Katie threw herself at the man called Thacker. Her booted foot found his shin, her teeth his hand, but before she could inflict any more damage, someone grabbed her from behind. Ripped from Thacker, she was thrown brutally into the dirt. The wind left her lungs and stones and rocks dug into her skin, but she barely noticed. Anger spun her around to face her assailant, and she found herself staring into the coal black eyes of another stranger.

"Thank you, Blake."

Katie looked from the man wearing scuffed boots, worn jeans and a tattered jacket to Thacker. He had a handkerchief out and was wrapping it around his hand. It was small satisfaction to realize she'd drawn blood. "You'll never get away with this!"

The cold, chiseled lines of Thacker's face moved into a chilling smile. "You won't be alive to watch us, but I can assure you that we will succeed. I'll even tell you how." He stooped before her. "When you're found dead with no apparent heirs, the bank is going to go a little crazy. The gold won't have all been checked and cleared, and the mortgage won't have been paid yet. We'll step in with an offer to buy. The bank will jump at the opportunity."

"But you won't be able to get the gold." The small victory brought a sense of great satisfaction.

He stood. "No, but your last thought will be of our surveyors coming to strip your beautiful rangeland of every mineral they can find. If we're lucky, we might even strike oil." He gestured to Blake, who immediately reached down to yank her to her feet.

She tried to twist away, but his grip was brutal. He was behind her and had both hands locked over her upper arms.

"Katie, please," Simon pleaded. "Do as they ask! Give them the ranch!"

She ignored him and spat at Thacker.

"Stupid move!" His hand swung up to deal a blow, but the slap never came. Instead his fingers curled into a fist, and he gave her a cold smile. "No, we can't have any unexplained marks on the face. Your death won't be questioned as long as it can easily be explained away." He gestured over the hill beyond Tyler's yard. "Blake's going to take you over to the cliff where you found the gold. It was easy enough to find with all the tracks you left. Once there, you're going to have an unfortunate fall. Simon, of course, will be left behind to run back and tell everyone all about it."

BLAKE FORCED HER FORWARD, and Travis watched Katie try to plant her feet to fight back. It was a useless effort against the man's greater strength. Travis gritted his teeth and hurried to slip down the incline behind Tyler's old barn.

Having arrived moments before, he hadn't been able to listen to what was being said, but it hadn't taken hearing for him to understand Katie was in trouble. She was outnumbered three to one, and he was the only one who could help her.

Ducking around the broken boards of the collapsed barn where he'd once found Tyler dead, Travis ran to the front of the building and pulled his Colt from its holster. He took a deep breath. He wasn't going to make the same mistake he had last time. Katie wasn't going to lose her life because of him.

He darted quickly across the short distance to the rear of the shack to take cover. There he edged to the corner and chanced a look around to the yard. Katie was being pushed into sight. Travis clenched his jaw and swung into the sunlight with his Colt raised and aimed. "You there! Let her go!"

"Travis!" Katie saw him, saw his gun and felt Blake release her right arm to grab at something inside his jacket. She started to twist in an attempt to break free. But, abruptly, she was shoved aside.

Staggering backward, she glimpsed the gun in Blake's hand, saw him point it at Travis and screamed as both guns exploded.

Stumbling to regain her balance, she saw Blake's body jerk. In panic she swung toward Travis, but before she could find him, she was grabbed again. Thacker caught her as Blake crumpled to the ground. Suddenly he had a gun, too, and was firing at Travis as he dragged her backward around the corner of the shack and out of sight.

Travis dived and rolled as bullets whistled over and around him. The first man was down and wasn't moving. Dead or unconscious, he was out of it. Travis started edging forward along the side of the shack. Katie had been taken away. He was going to get her back.

Katie tried to break Thacker's grip. Her foot found his shin. He yelled and raised his hand to hit her with the revolver, but Simon lurched forward to grab. Thacker's arm.

Caught between the struggling men, Katie was knocked aside. She tripped and stumbled to the ground as Thacker's gun unexpectedly went off. The bullet ripped into her shoulder, and she cried out in pain.

Travis jumped around the corner at the sound and saw Katie lying in the dirt. Blood stained her blouse, but she was up and conscious, as were the two men fighting. As he watched, the stranger broke free from Simon, lifted his gun and fired point-blank into the older man's chest.

"You!"

Thacker swung at the call. Simon was falling away from him, dead or dying. But even though Thacker had his gun up and level, Travis's Colt was already aimed. The big gun kicked, and Thacker was thrown backward by the bullet's impact.

Katie screamed as he staggered her way. His face held shock, his eyes death. A gaping hole had appeared in his shirt, and blood was spilling from it. She watched in horror as his knees collapsed and frantically rolled away as he started to fall.

Thacker's body hit the ground beside her, and Katie cringed from it. Holding her throbbing shoulder and with tears burning her eyes, she twisted away to find Travis. He was standing beside the shack with the still-smoking gun in his hand. Her eyes met his in mute relief and agony, but a movement behind him caught her attention. She looked away to see Blake up on his knees with a gun pointed at Travis's back. She screamed.

Even as Travis whirled, he heard the gun boom. The Colt answered, but he couldn't dodge and shoot, too. The bullet caught, stung and spun him around. Travis fought to keep his feet, but they went out from under him. And, as the ground reached up to grab him, he heard Katie's sobbing cry.

Chapter Fifteen

Katie stood staring at the tombstone emblazoned with the name Travis McCord. Beneath it were the words Friend and Sheriff. Tears burned her eyes, and she put a hand on the sling cradling her arm. A dull ache throbbed in her shoulder, but she barely felt it. The real pain was in her heart.

A sound came from behind her, and she turned to watch a man walk toward her. He had a bouquet of flowers in his hand. She smiled at the gesture, and lifted her eyes to his. "A remembrance?"

"Molly always liked flowers."

Katie watched Travis stoop to place the flowers on the grave of Molly Hunnicutt that lay so close to the one made for him over a hundred years before. The ache in her chest contracted again. She'd come so close to losing him just as he'd lost Molly. He stood again, and Katie slipped her hand into his. It was warm and strong.

He grinned at her. "We make quite a pair."

She laughed as he wiggled his fingers inside his sling. Each of them carried scars from the battle over the ranch. Each had a bullet wound in the shoulder.

The only difference was which side of their body had been injured. Her right arm was free as was his left.

"Ready to go?"

She nodded and turned with him toward the deserted streets of Eagle River beyond the cemetery. The old town hadn't seemed to have aged much since she'd seen it last, but Katie felt she had. Her life had changed dramatically in a matter of weeks, but it was the grief and fear of the past few days she wasn't sure she'd ever get over.

The discovery that both her mother and foreman had been murdered, the confession of Simon to theft and fraud, the threats and innuendos of Thacker, and the near loss of the man she'd grown to love. It was all too overwhelming. Hard to comprehend and accept. She'd had nightmares about the events leading to that final confrontation at Tyler Fenton's shack, and in her mind's eye she'd seen Travis turn again and again to face that final bullet.

If Travis hadn't seen the look in her eyes and followed her gaze over his shoulder, he surely would have died. For Blake had already been squeezing the trigger when Travis had turned to see what she had seen, and the move had saved his life. Instead of being killed as intended, he'd only been wounded, but the terror she'd felt as he'd fallen was still with her because he had landed almost exactly where he'd been found dead a hundred years before. History had nearly repeated itself.

Somehow Simon had still been breathing when she'd gotten to him. The light had been fading from his eyes as the blood had drained from his body, but he'd lived long enough to beg her forgiveness.

The radio in the back of the Jeep was how she and Travis had managed to call for help. Both bleeding and in pain, it had seemed like days before the deputies had finally arrived to take them to the hospital in Hancock, where they'd had to stay overnight. But rest had come only after their statements about what had happened had been given to the sheriff.

For Katie, all the details had poured out in a tidal wave of emotion, and she hadn't remembered Helen Henry until the next day. Given the chance, Katie would have tried to save Helen from the pain of the truth. But, accident or not, the tragedy and senselessness of Bill Henry's death had already been experienced. The news behind her husband's passing could bring no more hurt than it had already.

Sent home to the ranch by the doctors the next morning, Katie had insisted Travis stay in one of the other bedrooms in the house, but fear had clutched her heart when, after only a day, the FBI had come to call. She'd been certain someone had tried to dig into Travis's past and found him lacking, but it hadn't been Travis they were after. It had been Thacker.

Apparently he had worked with a certain man in Las Vegas who had been under surveillance. At the same time Thacker had been dying, his boss had been caught taking the bait of a carefully planned trap and would be spending the next twenty years in a jail cell.

Katie's worry that the federal agents would be looking into Travis's past proved groundless. They'd only been concerned with his corroboration of her story of what had occurred. She'd been asked nothing about Travis, who had suddenly found, of all things, a driver's license with a new birth date on it in his wallet. It seemed the past had managed to right it-self.

"I've been thinking," she told him as they walked down the hill from the cemetery to the deserted ghost town's streets. "Now that I have money, maybe I can help preserve Eagle River."

Travis's eyes met hers in startled surprise.

"There are a lot of ghost towns in Montana, but none of them mean as much to me as this one does. And," she said as they reached the Jeep, "I have an expert who can help me publish a book all about it."

He grinned and stopped beside her. "No one will ever believe it."

"So? Everyone else will call it fiction, but we'll know the truth. Besides, it's a fitting tribute to Tyler, seeing as how he made us rich."

"Us? Is that a proposal?"

She sighed. "You're awful slow at making one, and people are going to talk, with you living with me up at the house."

"Only if they know what we're doing up there," he told her as he pulled her against him. "Have you told anybody?"

Her face flushed with embarrassed heat as she avoided his steady gaze. "I didn't have to. Helen helps to change the beds. When only one's been slept in…"

"She won't tell anyone. But," he said as Katie's eyes lifted to his, "I did talk to Mike."

"You didn't tell him—"

"I asked if he'd be my best man."

Katie's face lit up. "You did?" But a frown imme-diately followed. "You asked him before you asked me?"

"I figured that way you couldn't say no, or you'd be seen as a tainted woman."

"Tainted woman!" She wrinkled her nose. "No one's used that phrase in about a hundred years."

He sighed. "That's what you'll get if you marry such an old man."

She grinned and lifted herself up on tiptoe to offer her lips to him. "You don't look so ancient."

Travis shifted his sling out of the way and pressed her against him for a lengthy kiss. When he finally raised his head to look down at her, his eyes were shining. "You don't look so bad yourself. Matter of fact, I've decided blue jeans are downright attractive on women. Much better than those old gingham gowns."

"Really? What else appeals to you about we modern women?"

"Woman. One is enough for me to handle."

"Good. Because this one isn't going to give you up."

His lips covered hers again in a promising embrace that neither one of them was in a hurry to end.

Where do you find hot Texas nights, smooth Texas charm and dangerously sexy cowboys?

Crystal Creek reverberates with the exciting rhythm of Texas. Each story features the rugged individuals who live and love in the Lone Star state.

"...a series that should hook any romance reader. Outstanding."
—*Rendezvous*

Praise for Margot Dalton's *Even the Nights Are Better*

"...every bit as engrossing as the others. Ms. Dalton wraps you in sentiment...this is a book you don't just read, you feel."
—*Rendezvous*

Praise for Margot Dalton's *New Way To Fly*

"This is a fine and fitting successor to the first ten Crystal Creek books. May they go on forever."
—*Rendezvous*

Don't miss the next book in this exciting series. Look for **NEVER GIVIN' UP ON LOVE** by MARGOT DALTON

Available in September wherever Harlequin books are sold.

This summer, come cruising with Harlequin Books!

PORTS
OF CALL

In July, August and September, excitement, danger and, of course, romance can be found in Lynn Leslie's exciting new miniseries PORTS OF CALL. Not only can you cruise the South Pacific, the Caribbean and the Nile, your journey will also take you to Harlequin Superromance®, Harlequin Intrigue® and Harlequin American Romance®.

- ◆ In July, cruise the South Pacific with SINGAPORE FLING, a Harlequin Superromance
- ◆ NIGHT OF THE NILE from Harlequin Intrigue will heat up your August
- ◆ September is the perfect month for CRUISIN' MR. DIAMOND from Harlequin American Romance

So, cruise through the summer with LYNN LESLIE and HARLEQUIN BOOKS!

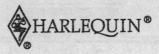

HARLEQUIN®

Weddings, Inc.

THE WEDDING GAMBLE
Muriel Jensen

Eternity, Massachusetts, was America's wedding town. Paul Bertrand knew this better than anyone—he never should have gotten soused at his friend's rowdy bachelor party. Next morning when he woke up, he found he'd somehow managed to say "I do"—to the woman he'd once jilted! And Christina Bowman had helped launch so many honeymoons, she knew just what to do on theirs!

THE WEDDING GAMBLE, available in September from American Romance, is the fourth book in Harlequin's new cross-line series, **WEDDINGS, INC.**

Be sure to look for the fifth book, **THE VENGEFUL GROOM,** by Sara Wood (Harlequin Presents #1692), coming in October.

HARLEQUIN

A M E R I C A N ✦ R O M A N C E®

A NEW STAR COMES OUT TO SHINE....

American Romance continues to search
the heavens for the best new talent...
the best new stories.

Join us next month when a new star
appears in the American Romance
constellation:

Kim Hansen
#548 TIME RAMBLER
August 1994

*Even in the shade of a broad-rimmed Stetson,
Eagle River's lanky sheriff had the bluest
eyes Katie Shannon had ever seen. But why
was he in the ghost town—a man who was
killed in a shoot-out one hundred years ago?*

RISING STAR

Be sure to Catch a "Rising Star"!

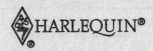

HARLEQUIN®

Don't miss these Harlequin favorites by some of our most
distinguished authors!
And now you can receive a discount by ordering two or more titles!

HT #25525	THE PERFECT HUSBAND by Kristine Rolofson	$2.99	☐
HT #25554	LOVERS' SECRETS by Glenda Sanders	$2.99	☐
HP #11577	THE STONE PRINCESS by Robyn Donald	$2.99	☐
HP #11554	SECRET ADMIRER by Susan Napier	$2.99	☐
HR #03277	THE LADY AND THE TOMCAT by Bethany Campbell	$2.99	☐
HR #03283	FOREIGN AFFAIR by Eva Rutland	$2.99	☐
HS #70529	KEEPING CHRISTMAS by Marisa Carroll	$3.39	☐
HS #70578	THE LAST BUCCANEER by Lynn Erickson	$3.50	☐
HI #22256	THRICE FAMILIAR by Caroline Burnes	$2.99	☐
HI #22238	PRESUMED GUILTY by Tess Gerritsen	$2.99	☐
HAR #16496	OH, YOU BEAUTIFUL DOLL by Judith Arnold	$3.50	☐
HAR #16510	WED AGAIN by Elda Minger	$3.50	☐
HH #28719	RACHEL by Lynda Trent	$3.99	☐
HH #28795	PIECES OF SKY by Marianne Willman	$3.99	☐

Harlequin Promotional Titles

#97122	LINGERING SHADOWS by Penny Jordan	$5.99	☐
	(limited quantities available on certain titles)		

	AMOUNT	$
DEDUCT:	10% DISCOUNT FOR 2+ BOOKS	$
	POSTAGE & HANDLING	$
	($1.00 for one book, 50¢ for each additional)	
	APPLICABLE TAXES*	$_____
	TOTAL PAYABLE	$_____
	(check or money order—please do not send cash)	

To order, complete this form and send it, along with a check or money order for the
total above, payable to Harlequin Books, to: **In the U.S.:** 3010 Walden Avenue,
P.O. Box 9047, Buffalo, NY 14269-9047; **In Canada:** P.O. Box 613, Fort Erie, Ontario,
L2A 5X3.

Name: _____

Address:_____City: _____

State/Prov.: _____ Zip/Postal Code: _____

*New York residents remit applicable sales taxes.
 Canadian residents remit applicable GST and provincial taxes..

HBACK-JS